*Other books by T.K. Galarneau ...*

A Cowboy Tradition: Poems from the Heart
Meadow Muffins in the Trail
Ruminations of an Old Woman
The Arrangement

# DUSTY ROSE, GUS & ME

## T.K GALARNEAU

GusGus Press ● Fairfield, California

978-1-949290-86-8 paperback

Cover Photo
by

Cover Design
by

GusGus Press
a division of
Bedazzled Ink Publishing Company
Fairfield, California
http://www.bedazzledink.com

*To Gwen Williams she helped me train Dusty.*
*I'm sure she is looking down on all of us chuckling at Gus's antics.*
*Both she and Dusty are together enjoying a nice leisurely trail ride.*
*Thank you Gwenny.*

# PART I

## CROSSIN' THE CREEK

As far as doin' all I asked
Ya never once refused a task
Was always proud as I could be
And when we rode I felt free

You began your life with a clean slate
With you and me, well it was fate
The Creator made sure I had a plan
Time together our lives would span

We had our ups and downs for sure
Many's a time you made my life pure
Hell when I taught you to cross the creek
I sure as hell didn't think you'd freak

But your reaction was a real surprise
Still given your disposition I surmised
You'd follow your ma just like a pup
Maybe an argument but you'd give up

Oh hell no! Not my Dusty Rose
I should have known and I suppose
I had it comin' for being plumb blind
For not knowin' what was in your mind.

I'd ponied you most all over the place
You followed politely and never raced
You picked your way over rocky trails
I turned you lose; you stayed on ma's tail

By the time a creek I introduced to you
You were eight months and this was new
Stout for sure; boy how you'd grown
How strong you were I should've known

By the edge of the creek we took a rest
I give you some time to do your best
To check out the water so you could see
There was no danger and ne'r you'd flee

I need not have worried; you wouldn't run
You just stood there you son of a gun
I spurred your ma, but you wouldn't budge
I swear to God you sure had a grudge

Against me for crossin' that creek was the last
Thing you would do, so just that fast
I dallied my rope and then I just dragged
Deep chestnut butt and then I sure bragged

"How do you like that?" I said with a grin
And just to be safe, I did it again
Once more, twice more, until you walked
Right through the creek not once did you balk.

As proud as punch I was with my filly
'Cause she never again acted so silly
And never again did she refuse to cross
Any water—guess she knew who was boss.

## GOIN' FOR A SWIM

When I was a youngin' I loved to swim
I spent my summers by the river's edge

I swam like a fish; I should have had gills.
Course I was human; water wasn't my home

The years passed by one by one; they piled one on the other.
Wasn't long 'til my swimmin' friends no longer stayed around.

I breathed, I slept, I dreamed; my friends were the equine kind.
Horses were a passion; the river a distant memory.

Til twenty years had come and gone 'tween youth and middle age
My swimmin' skills confounded me; I'd forgotten all I knew

So the last time I went swimmin' I sure 'nough danged near drowned
Since I could go out ridin' and I could stay plum dry; horses were my
high.

Now I never think of water much 'cept when I need a drink
Til on a sunny August day my thinkin' surely changed.

Dusty and I were ridin' 'long the irrigation ditch
The ride was pleasant my pony was workin' well.

I was chattin' with a friend of mine when ev'rthin' turned sour
Dusty stopped so quick you'da thought she'd seen a bear.

She wouldn't go no further; she simply stopped and stared.
The thing was big and bright and blue; a brand new water pump.

Just ten short feet in front of her; you'd think that she'd go by.
No such luck her feet were stuck; we sure was in a bind.

I knew that she could back up quick, but this was record time.
We was headin' straight into the drink; that canal just feet behind.

It wasn't deep, but it sure was wet; I nearly lost my mind.
You'd think I'd worry 'bout myself or my pony's welfare too.

Perhaps my friend was worried too that I had met my end
Nope I thought about my saddle 'cause it was danged near new.

I took a bit to look around; I checked from stem to stern
There wasn't nothin' broken and Dusty wasn't lame.

First thing we needed was a plan on how to pull us out.
The sides were slick and muddy; my feet could not take hold.

Roy Rogers, he had Trigger; my friend well not so much.
Still her Killian was a p'lice horse; he'd seen most ev'rthin'.

Now those Saturday morning serials were rattlin' in my brain
'Cause I just said, "Barb I'll bet Killian can pull me outta here."

Barb musta thought I'd lost my mind, or my head had took a whack.
"Are you sure that this will work; cause we don't have no rope."

"Oh sucks," said I. "Don't need no rope; hook the rein into the halter."
If I had time to think a while I might have changed my mind.

"Okay," said Barb. "You're all hooked up, now what am I to do?"
Her reins were kinda skinny; I hoped they'd hold my weight.

"Well toss me down the other end and have your horse back up.
This should have been a piece of cake, why Roy did it all the time."

Well sure enough he surprised us both, ol Killian backed up true.
My plan was workin' like I'd hoped, I was risin' from the drink.

I'll never know if Killian would have pulled me all plum out.
'Cause next thing that I knew was six hands a grabbin' me.

The ranch hand on the place next door saw the fix that I was in
He came along with help enough to pull me to dry land.

I was out but not my horse, Dusty was still a swimmin' round.
Her rein was locked up in my grasp; there's no way I'da let go.

"Well," I mused. "Let's just see if she can climb on out.
So come on girl get on up, you can't stay there all day."

Sure enough she scrambled out, and shook herself near clean.
No worse for wear, we thanked the boys; and walked back to the barn.

A mud bath never was my thing, but this day I sure I had one
From head to toe there weren't one spot that wasn't colored brown.

It's been a while since our little swim, and I learned one thing for sure.
If you ever encounter a bear that's blue go the other way around.

# HOO DOO LAKE: THE FALL

For some folks a saddle's a must,
For others it's bareback or bust.

As for myself, I need the leather
My rhyme will prove altogether

What I need is a saddle a little wider
'Cause plainly put I ain't no bronc rider

My friend and me loaded up our ponies
To Hoo Doo Lake, where the trails are stony

We'd planned a trip to last four days
And the weather just plumb amazed

Us both 'cause there was times rain
Poured down in sheets to our disdain

And left us soaked down to the skin
Our water proof tents could not begin

To turn the tide of that gall darn water
That made our camp unfit for a squatter

Hey! I've left the trail from where I began
Had no complaints the weather was grand

We rode the trails 'til we had our fill
A flowing stream like a sleeping pill

Put us to sleep in the cool night air
Bedrolls laid out under a sky I swear

Full of stars the Creator threw each one
In a special spot and when He was done

He threw in the moon to light our camp
Like the kind of glow from a neon lamp.

Gosh darn! once again like an ornery stray
From my original story I've veered away

I was talkin' 'bout a saddle I needed to ride
Dusty Rose my good horse right by my side.

Ready to leave; we'd packed up our gear
Dusty and I to the creek cold and clear

We walked quite a piece for a last long drink
And while she was drinking I started to think

Why walk her back when I could easily ride
Her back to camp on her bare chestnut hide.

I should have known better 'cause I'll tell you why
Dusty was built like a barrel; withers she was shy
Of and her hide was so tight, no grip could be had
I scrambled aboard sitting on an equine launch pad.

A launch was overstated 'cause to tell the truth
I had never rode bareback even in my youth

Bound and determined to ride back to camp
Around her round barrel, my legs I did clamp

I squeezed my legs gently and asked her to turn
But in less than a second a hard lesson I learned

One small step was all it took and I began to slip
Off I tumbled down to the ground when I lost my grip

Dusty stood there lookin' down at me; in her eyes
I could see she thought I had sure been unwise

To try and ride without a saddle to hold
Never try doing something and being so bold

That common sense would surely overrule
A smart human being from being a fool.

That may be so; I made a mistake
Lucky all I got was a little backache.

I gathered up what was left of my pride
Grabbed Dusty's lead and dared not ride

Back to camp, loaded up my laughin' mare
With best kept secrets not meant to share.

# THE BABY SITTER

It's been a while since rode
But her seat is pert near true.
Her legs they go this way and that,
Still by golly she sure does try.

Her cuing time still needs some work,
The horse works faster than she.
The horse is trained and finely tuned.
She thinks she knows the rules.

Now don't you think I findin' fault
Cause most every rider knows
We've all been through the ridin' blues
The beginnin's always tough.

The most important thing to have
'Sides confidence in your skills,
Is a horse that's been around the block
They're "baby sitters" by trade.

Now there is one partic'lar horse
That fits the bill just fine.
She's comin' on near twenty-two
And she's honest as she's true.

True she has a "*cantanktuous*" side,
A peppermint will smooth that out.
She knows her leads and how to turn
She'll still stop on a dime.

She's slowed a bit these past few years,
And she's nearly blind in her right eye.
She limps a bit, but when warmed up
She collects up smooth as silk.

Her silky liver chestnut hide
Is showin' flecks of white.
Right now she looks a little rough,
She's grown her winter fur.

But in the spring she'll slick right up.
You can't tell she's twenty-two.
She'll run and buck just like she's young.
She's hidin' a trick or two.

When she was young we'd gather cows,
We'd even cut a few.
She's been down trails that made you pray
Yet she'd never miss a step.

The time has come to slow up some,
She's surely paid her dues.
The rough and ready saddle colt
Is due some long slack time.

So let's go back up to the start,
It's time to tell the tale.
The "baby sitter's" latest charge
Is waitin' at the rail.

## YA FINALLY GOT A GOOD HORSE

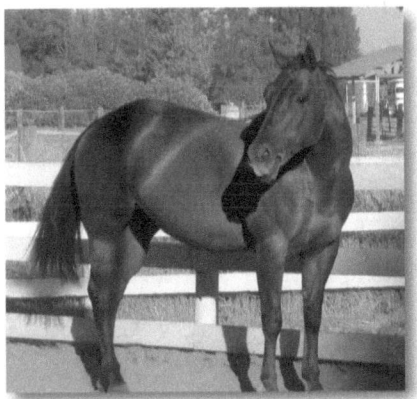

I raised my filly from foal to mare
I could not have been more proud.
She was sure a stout young thing
No cow could ever get by her.

Everyone who watched her work
Thought she would surely be
A gall darn good cow horse
When she was fully grown.

I loved her to death for ya see
She was a whole lot like me
Dusty and I saw life the same
Temperaments were just alike

Across the west the Quarter Horse
Takes most all of the ranching jobs
To some there ain't nothin' else
Appys and Paints need not apply.

I'd been known to ride them Apps
Although I had a quarter or two
Seemed to me a horse was a horse
As long as he had the right aptitude.

*T. K. Galarneau*

Still to folks here 'bouts an Appy
Ain't no kinda horse a'tall
Why you'd think they had a disease
Appy spots might rub off on their horse.

So I wasn't surprised when my friends
Applauded when I came up on my mare.
She was a beautiful liver chestnut;
Weren't a single spot to be found.

Looks can be deceiving we know
And folks were not aware that
The parents of my trusty mare
Were Appys through and through

My good old filly didn't color
She was as solid as she could be
I thought I might get some white
Year followed year without no change

I would have liked to have some spots
But I could never ever complain
Dusty Rose was the finest horse
I ever had the pleasure to ride.

# PART II

## A CLOSE SHAVE

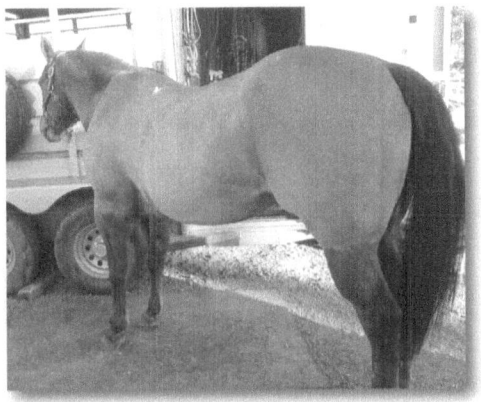

You were a hairy beast that's true
All winter long your hair sure grew
I'd stick my finger to the second knuckle
'Fore I'd hit a rib; I'd have to chuckle

Come spring I'd brush and brush some more
I would work all day 'til my arm was sore
Finally, after I'd had enough of Appy hair
I took a step back and at the floor I stared

There was hair enough for more than one
Horse or maybe two; brushin' sure wasn't fun
My dad would say, " . . . work smart not hard."
I was pretty sure Dusty wouldn't be scarred

If I used good sense and the clippers I bought
To rid us both of her winter coat I thought
She'd sure 'nough be a pretty slick Appy
And I surmised to say we'd both be happy

So to work I went first I bathed and dried
A winter coat right down to the hide.
Once I was sure the dam dirt was all gone
I said a pray when the clippers came on.

To my surprise and relief my girl was quiet
I wasn't too sure she might cause a riot
But true to her nature she took in stride
Almost every darn thing on her I tried

When the clippers got hot we took a break
I wasn't too sure how long this would take
I started in back and worked to the front
If I hit a tricky spot, she'd only just grunt

After an hour or two I'd finished the job
Good thing too; for my fingers did throb
For my first body clip I think I gave
This Appy mare a pretty close shave.

## A Gift from God

On April 18, 1990,
A filly hit the ground.
She was s'posed to be all spotted
But ne'ry a spot did I find.

I called her Ha Dar's Dusty Rose
'Cause of her colored coat.
There were no spots,
But still in all her color was unique.

She was my first don't ya see
Cause all my life it used to be
Someone's problems I would get
Still I'd train 'em you can bet.

In fact her ma was just like that
She'd been abused and mostly used
To show her colorful Appy hide
But very rarely did they ride.

I took her home and raised her up
She'd cut and hike but no one liked
The fact that she was an App
Them quarter horse folks can shut their yap.

But I digress a blessin' is my tale
When Dusty hit the ground
She rolled around and then jumped up
I was as proud as any mother could be

I sold her mom and she's passed on
Dusty and I have been partners for years
Twenty-three seems a long time to me
And when I'm down, alone, or just bummed

I look in her eyes and what do I see?
 A blessing from God staring back at me. Dusty Rose

# DUSTY ROSE

I can't believe it's been this long,
These twenty years have passed.
The bond we share is still as strong,
Our friendship's unsurpassed.

A filly came one early morn,
When spring was still so young.
Her ma she looked a might forlorn,
Her head on me she hung.

I checked her good before she stood,
She looked like she was healthy.
That filly she was packaged good,
I knew she'd be trustworthy.

The only thing I couldn't see,
She should have had so many.
'Course there's not a guarantee,
There'd be white spots a plenty.

But since her ma and pa had spots,
You'd think that it should follow.
Their baby'd hit a big jackpot,
My pride I'd have to swallow.

She was as feisty as could be,
She thought she'd rule the roost.
Until she bit me on the knee,
A rebuff that produced!

Once she knew I was the boss,
For learnin' she was ready.
I never had to get too cross,
We took it slow and steady.

She was a pretty lil thing,
Her hide a pale rose.
Standin' in the early spring,
She struck the cutest pose.

In the sun a shinin' bright,
Her reflection it did show.
The palest color in the light,
Just like a dusty rose.

Seasons come and seasons go,
One thing is always constant.
Our attitudes they go to show,
We're just so co- dependent.

We galloped over rollin' hills,
The canyons steep were awful deep.
Our rides provided chills and thrills,
I'm sure would scare a big horn sheep.

A bit of this a bit of that,
We've tried most ever'thin'.
A hundred miles to Joseph Flats,
We rode 'long side a buckskin.

We took up cuttin' early on,
She caught on pretty fast.
The cattle she attacked head-on,
All comers she outclassed.

We tried a little reinin',
But that she couldn't do.
Her feet they took to floppin'
Her legs were all askew.

We even showed a time or two,
They called 'em workin' ranch.
But she could never get the clue,
Why we could not advance.

Cuz when a horse just cut her off,
She got a might perturbed.
She'd strike out with a left hind hoof,
That left the judge disturbed.

Our plan for showin' was cut short,
Still there's plenty left you see.
We've had more fun I can report,
But shows weren't meant to be.

We've ridden after cattle,
We've traveled many miles.
There's never been a battle,
Mostly there've been smiles.

That's not to say she's never crossed,
My good side now and then.
Why Dusty Rose that's me you tossed,
Across the gall darn pen.

Now we're gettin' older,
Some aches and pains we got.
Right now she's gettin' sounder,
But her owner's knees are shot.

Horace Greeley he once said,
"Go west my fine young friend."
I loaded up the flatbed,
I joined a growing trend.

We moved to Californie,
We're out here in the sun.
Dusty's home don't come for free.
But we're havin' lots of fun.

We hit a major speed bump,
Along the road of life.
Dusty's head it took a thump,
That caused a lot of strife.

The docs up there in Davis,
Appraised the accident,
There's gonna be some numbness,
Around the bone fragments.

She had a stall for just one night,
Then I could bring her home.
To look at her it caused me fright,
I shook down to my bones.

Dusty Rose came through it,
With the tiniest of scars.
She's got an awful lot of grit,
But I cried through the bars.

Since she's healed up just fine,
We're on the downhill slide.
We haven't rid no steep inclines,
We're savin' both our hides.

I guess we have retired,
We're takin' things real slow.
We just ain't that hardwired,
To be puttin' on a show.

There's gonna come a day I know,
When our two trails will part.
Yet our bond will surely grow,
She'll never leave my heart.

# I Can Never Say Goodbye

How in the world do you say goodbye
To a twenty-five-year-old standby?

From foal to weanling to filly to mare,
No matter the weather she was there.

She wasn't "just a horse" you see,
She was my friend as true any could be.

I never raised my own horse before.
From birth to death I didn't need more.

She was honest and true blue
There was nothin' she wouldn't do.

We cut, we reined; we covered the mountains.
Where ever I'd point, she was sure game.

Fact there were times, boy you can bet
There's places we went we sure did get wet!

Not once did she balk, not once did she shy,
No matter the trail I was sure we'd get by.

But time marches on and we both did succumb
Age and arthritis, yep old we'd become.

Our rides were confined to the straight and narrow
No mountains high, trails were straight as an arrow.

Still she could stop on a dime and give you change
Every now and then we'd work on the range.

She liked chasing cows and checking fence
But down in CA weren't no call for cow sense.

She stayed in her pasture and ate sweet grass
In fact she was happy and it came to pass,

One night in late winter she plopped down to roll
She should have known better when she was a foal

Into the fence in one fail swoop she caught one hind foot
She thrashed and rolled but she was hard put

To get herself free; the damage was done
When she got up she knew the end had begun.

When I got the call the one unexpected
My friend was in peril left unprotected.

At Davis they worked to save my friend
The vets' skill was stunnin', but in the end

The verdict was grim and her chances were slim.
She wanted to live but the pain was too much.

The OR suite it was sterile and cold,
A life was snuffed out; more priceless than gold.

What could I say to my partner my friend
I had never prepared for her life to end.

I cried and I pleaded to the Creator above
I knew in my heart the last gift of love

Was for me to let her go to the Lord
Where her soul'd be restored.

I spread her ashes to the winds
Where eternity begins.

Like the Greek's Elysian Fields
All her wounds would be healed.

She' workin' God's cattle
The end of life's battles.

And when it's my time
To end life's climb.

We'll be united again
My partner and friend.

## WHATCHA DOIN?

It was a year ago today.
You chose to go away.
I cried and mourned,
I cursed the day you were born.

The pain was more than I could bare.
I'd go to the barn but you weren't there.
But with time comes retrospect,
The tears are coming less and less.
Now only happy times come to mind
Like that rocky hill we used to climb
As you climbed you'd grunt and groan
You'd thought I'd beat you to the bone.

I had plans when I quit workin'
You and I would be out searchin'
All day long we would stay
Anywhere that we could play

You'd teach ol' Gus the ropes
To get around a slippery slope.
You would be my pony horse.
I'll have to change my plans of course.

These days I sit and wonder
What yer doin' way up yonder?
Does God have cattle you can work?
I bet you drive Him plumb berserk.

The Good Lord's patience has no bounds
Still a year with you He prob'ly come unwound.
'Cause you've been known to pitch a fit
With you there's times I'd damn near quit.

In my mind's eye I see vast green valleys
With runnin' streams where you could dally
You could wander where you will
All day long you'd eat your fill.

You've got company that's for sure
Buzzard and Blue are up there too.
'Tween the Lord and a dang good mare
Will keep watch of all in their care.

I sure miss the times we had
But I can't really feel all that bad
I know you've earned the peace
And quiet of your resting place.

# PART IIII

## A Hundred Miles

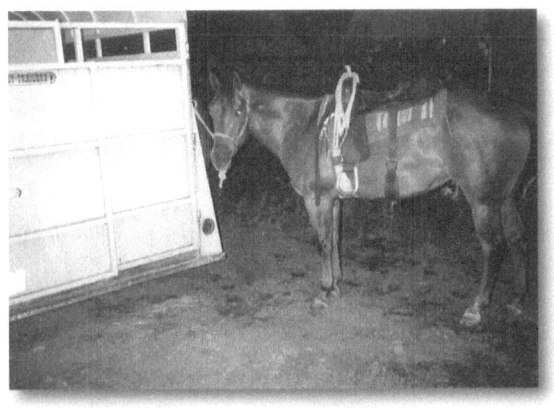

DUSTY WAS STILL very young, just four years old. There isn't anything too unusual for turning another year old except that this year particular year, 1994, the Asotin County Fair was celebrating its fiftieth year. To commemorate the occasion, the fair board came up with the idea of organizing a trail ride from Asotin, Washington to Joseph, Oregon . . . some one hundred miles southwest . . . as the crow flies. The organizers coincided the ride with Chief Joseph Days and all of the trail riders would ride through town in the parade . . . nearly 135 people.

My friend decided that it was something we oughta do. I was a little concerned that Dusty was still young and had never done such a long ride, although I had ridden her out on mountain trails for the past year, these were short rides. We'd start out early in the day and ride ten or twelve miles, then head back to the trailer. The other fly in the ointment, in my view, was that Joseph Days were celebrated the last weekend in July. In this part of the country, southwestern Washington and northeastern Oregon, the temperatures can reach the triple digits, not the most comfortable riding weather . . . in my estimation, at least. The fair officials had managed to announce the ride well in advance of the departure time, so there was plenty of time to get horse and rider in shape for an eight-hour-a-day, seven-day ride. Okay, I'll concede that at least. Getting Dusty in shape wouldn't be a problem. There were other considerations however, the least of which was the cost. I always wanted to ride the Chief Joseph Trail Ride (after all I did own an Appy) but the cost was prohibitive. The Asotin County Ride would be relatively cheap . . . $165.00. Included were meals and feed for the horses. There'd be entertainment in the evenings and a converted stock horse trailer would provide showers. I could do that.

In retrospect, I probably should have stayed home. A good friend had traveled all the way to Colorado and made a similar ride. Called "Gentlemen on Horseback," there were some one hundred and fifty riders and this ride was set up just like the Asotin ride. When I asked him how he enjoyed the ride he said, " . . . it was something I always wanted to do, but would never do again." Talk about foreshadowing! But the decision was made; I didn't feel like I could back out.

We set about getting the horses in shape; every day for the next six months we would ride the canyons up Asotin Creek. Then at least twice a week we'd haul up to the mountains or over to Hellsgate Park and ride the hills. Not only did Dusty get in the best shape of her life, so did I; I lost about thirty-five pounds. I had just purchased a new (to me; already broke in) cutting saddle which fit her well and for the next six months, with all that riding, there were no signs of an ill fit. Again, a little foreshadowing. Dusty's only fault was she was "mutton withered." Simply put, she didn't have a prominent set of withers to hold a saddle and this made her susceptible to saddle sores. I was very careful about choosing saddles to fit her for that very reason. Fifteen years later, I finally had enough money to splurge on a custom-made saddle for her.))


THE APPOINTED DAY arrived, and Dusty and I found ourselves at the ride staging area at the Asotin County Fairgrounds. Good thing I was a morning person and used to getting up at five a.m. because everyone was to arrive by six for breakfast and the obligatory group picture. I decided to ride my mare in a hackamore and mecate; it would be easier for her to graze and drink during breaks on the trail. She worked really well and never fought her head at all. Today was a little different. She had never been in a bunch numbering a hundred and thirty-five horses, people, and commotion before today. She was a bit nervous and (admittedly so was I) tossed her head frequently. Oh yay! Remember about what my friend said about his ride? Forewarned is forearmed. Oh well, in for a penny, in for a pound.

Among the hundred and thirty-five riders, probably half were show people (no offense) whose horses wouldn't drink if they couldn't see the bottom of their water trough. Most of these show horses had never been out on the trail and were decidedly out of shape. (Remember when I mentioned the heat earlier? More about that later.) To add to the cacophony around us, these riders were ill-mannered and hadn't the least idea about being in a large group. My friend and I decided the two safest places to be, for the first day at least, would be in the very front, or the very back. We ended up somewhere near the end twenty horses up. By mid-morning, we decided the back wasn't good 'cause our horses were used to riding at a faster pace than western pleasure horses. So when the trail widened out, we hot footed it up toward the front. We found some of our ranching friends whose horses were used to traveling at a good clip checking cattle.

"We wondered how long you'd last back there, Terrie," old man Hollenbeck remarked. "How's your mare likin' this?"

"Holy crap," I replied. "Wouldn't you think people would have gotten their horses in better shape before they decided to go on a hundred-mile trail ride?"

"Why would you think that?" The old man chuckled. "Heck as long as they have plenty of booze, they're good to go."

In deference to the horse show people, there wasn't any booze allowed until evening camp was set up. Old man Hollenbeck was a crotchety old man who had no use for show people . . . period. He thought showing was a waste of a good horse. We chatted a bit more, then I decided to be neighborly and find some other folks I knew.

"Keep your powder dry," I called. "Maybe I'll see you this evening."

"Oh hell," the old man cried, "they wouldn't let me bring my gun either."

Oh God, I thought. They sure don't make 'em like that anymore. There were a couple of officers from the Lewis-Clark Saddle Club, of which I was a member. The club had been toying with the idea of sponsoring a trail ride so they chose to come along to see what such a ride would be like.

"Hey, Larry," I said. "What do you think about the ride? You think the saddle club can handle a ride like this?"

"I don't see why not," he replied. "Choosing a route and getting permission from the BLM and private landowners would be the first thing."

"That's a little complicated and involved isn't it?" I asked.

"Not really. The toughest thing for us would be to get enough people to ride so the thing is cost effective. The more people, the lower the fee," Larry said.

I left Larry to stew over his trail ride and I went to look up my friend. She had managed to find a friend or two to ride with, but things weren't going too well. Her big old Appy gelding was great in the hills, could cut a cow, and drag calves to the branding fire. He had a great disposition . . . not flighty or obnoxious . . . he'd work all day without complaint, but he wanted to be home at night. We stopped in the shade for our lunch when Beth voiced her concerns.

"I'm hoping Red will be okay tonight tied to the trailer," she said. "You know he hates being away from home at night. I'm wondering now if I was a bit hasty coming on this ride."

God, I thought. Fine time to worry about that now.

"Oh, he should be okay," I reassured Beth. "He and Dusty get along fine. As long as he has her for company, I think things will work out. Besides, after today's ride, he'll be too pooped to mess around." Famous last words.

We finished lunch and tightened our cinches and everyone mounted and headed on up the trail. I knew the pooped part of my message to Beth was a bunch of hooey. Red and Dusty were in such good shape and the slow pace of this ride wouldn't begin to tire them out. Ya couldn't say the same for a bunch of the other riders. Their horses were out of shape and even the slow pace was too much for them. Many of the show ponies were a huffin' and a puffin'. Heck, Red and Dusty had barely broke a sweat. The weather forecast for the week was for unseasonably warm temperatures, which meant, for July, we were all going to cook! While today wasn't too bad (85 degrees), by mid-week the temperatures were supposed to be triple digits. Good thing there was a vet along on this ride; I had a feeling there were folks who were going to need him.

THE FIRST DAY was coming to a close. The first night's camp site was just ahead. The organizers had gotten permission to cross private land, and we had the advantage of being able to use the rancher's stock pond. Beth and I unsaddled our horses and found where Ben, Beth's husband, had parked the rig. Everyone had support people (they traveled by road) who hauled all your gear: tents, clothes, etc. The trail organizers provided the feed, which had to be Oregon hay, purchased in Oregon. Oregonians were picky about invasive weeds that might come into their state by way of out of state hay. I can't say I blamed them . . . there was virtually no "yellow star thistle" in Oregon. While this noxious weed had virtually taken over most of the Pacific Northwest. I fought it at my place, so I know how hard it is to control the stuff once it takes root.

Anyway, Ben found a place out of the way of other riders. We had to hike some up to the stage area and supper, but we were also away from the rowdy drinkers that wanted to party. They'd be sorry in the morning. We unsaddled, then took the horses to the pond to get a good long drink. Fortunately, there were plenty of opportunities for the horses to drink throughout the day and our horses were quite comfortable drinking out of a creek or pond. They figured water is water and they'd best take a drink when they could. We tied them up, hung the hay nets, and let them be. I was ready for a shower. I grabbed my soap, clean underwear, shorts, sneakers, and a shirt and waited my turn. When I was cleaned up, I headed for a camp chair and a cold drink.

Once everyone had gotten horses, gear, and themselves cared for, the dinner bell rang. Steak, corn, beans, and biscuits was the fare. For dessert, apple turnovers . . . pretty darn good. There was soda, water, and beer to wash everything down. After dinner, we enjoyed cowboy music and poetry. People wandered around getting acquainted, but mostly people sat quietly: everyone was pretty tired from the first day's ride.

Beth, Ben, and I sat by a campfire and chilled. Beth was still worried about Red. I figured if left to his own devices, he'd be fine. Ben checked on him before we bedded down and he seemed fine, at least for the present. Several hours into the night, around two or so, we were awoken by banging and clanging at the trailer. There was Red all tangled up, his halter half off. He had rubbed and worked until he had nearly freed himself. In the process, rather than freeing himself, he only entangled himself in his lead rope. He'd also dug a hole dang near to China. He was plumb soaked from his efforts, so there was nothing for it, but to walk him 'til he dried, then take him home in the morning. Beth thought she'd put him left untied in the trailer; maybe he'd feel a little safer. He was quiet for about five minutes, then he started stomping. Ben decided, dark or not, to take him home immediately. We took my gear out of the trailer, and I'd put it on the truck with everyone else's belongings. We agreed Ben and Beth would pick me up in Joseph at the end of the ride. So much for our mutual vacation. I could see Beth was really disappointed; after all this was her idea. She wanted to do the ride more than I did. I was just coming along for the ride, no pun intended.

"Dang," I said. "I'm sorry about this, Beth. I can only imagine how bummed you must be."

"Yeah," Beth sighed, "I kinda thought this might happen, but I figured riding all day Red would be too tuckered to fool around at night. I didn't plan on such a slow pace though."

"That's for dam sure," I replied. "Our horses are in way too gooda shape to be traveling this slowly. I guess the leaders have to accommodate all the horses who are out of shape."

Then I had a thought.

"Ya know," I mused. "We could take turns . . . alternate days on Dusty, so at least you could ride some of the time."

"Thanks for the offer," Beth sighed, "but that's not fair to you."

"Hey," I stated. "Don't matter to me. I just came along for the ride and Dusty sure as hell won't care. I mean you paid for the chance to do this and I'll bet the management won't refund you your money. Or maybe they would; you could ask."

"That's an idea," Beth said. "I'll check into that. Maybe we'll just come along for the social aspect."

"You're sure as hell more socially inclined than I am." I laughed. "The social aspect is the one drawback to this whole ride. You decide what you want to do and I'll either see you at the end of the day tomorrow or in Joseph on the weekend."

I helped them get Red in the trailer and get Beth's gear put away.

"Okay," Beth whispered. "You'd better get some sleep. Ya know we probably will take care of things at home and see you on the weekend."

Beth was really depressed.

"Well," I reiterated. "My offer still goes."

Next morning, which came rather quickly with only three or four hours of sleep, I gathered up my gear and took everything to the truck. I didn't particularly want to sleep on the cold ground without my tent or bedroll. And I didn't particularly want to wear the same clothes for the rest of the week, so I made sure to stow my possibles carefully where they wouldn't be left behind. I ran into old man Hollenbeck on the way to breakfast.

"What happened to your riding partner?" the old man growled.

"Oh Red couldn't stand to be away from home," I laughed, "so Beth and Ben took him home. I guess I'm on my own until the weekend and they'll meet me in Joseph. Otherwise Dusty will have to haul me home. That would be a helluva trip, huh?"

Hollenbeck scratched his grizzled, grey stubble thoughtfully. "Why didn't she bring her mare on this trip? She's sure enough a good trail horse, ain't she?"

"Yes, she is," I replied, "but she's bred and Beth didn't want to take the risk of stressing her and maybe lose the foal."

"Oh hell," Hollenbeck snorted. "That mare better be tougher than that or she ain't much of a horse."

Yeah, easy for you to say, I thought. She isn't his mare.

"Well," I mused. "She owns the mare, and Beth's the one who has to do what she thinks is best. I don't know if I would have brought Alee while she was bred."

"Oh, hell," the old man said, "you cut cattle on Alee right up until she foaled. Didn't hurt her."

"Geez, man," I countered. "I rode Alee for short periods and the weather was a whole lot cooler. That's a big difference."

Hollenbeck just shook his head and walked away. There's no arguing with that man.

Back out on the trail, Dusty stepped right out. We had gotten the roughest part of the trip out of the way . . . descending the canyon down to the Grand Ronde River was no picnic. The trail wound mostly through shale and loose sharp rock that was slippery as hell. Dusty emerged unscathed except for a small cut on her fetlock. A long soak in the river took care of that. The ascent up the other side of the canyon was a whole lot easier and once we were on top, the trail widened onto the prairie and a much nicer ride. Now if I could just rid myself of the fool woman who kept riding up on Dusty's butt, I'd be in heaven. (Dusty never once offered to kick before this ride. After the ride, well, that's a whole 'nother story. If a horse got too close, she'd fire away. I learned to read her body language pretty well, so I could stop her

before she'd kick. But I never completely cured her of that nasty habit.)
I tried to be polite and warned this idiot of the consequences of riding
too close to another horse, but she never got the message. I tried riding
in front, in the rear, in the middle, and along either side of the bunch.
Somehow this woman always found me. I even tried to hide between
horses; nothing seemed to work.

"What is it with that lady?" one rider asked, "Why is she tailgating
you so much?"

"Oh man." I sighed. "I wish I knew. I've been polite in asking her to
back off, but she just doesn't get it. I guess now I'll have to be plumb
rude."

One of my friends from the saddle club heard our conversation.

"Hey Terrie." Kathy laughed. "That shouldn't be hard for you."

"Very funny," I retorted. "Be careful how you talk to me or I'll put
that lady on your tail."

"No thanks," Kathy replied, "but you better get ready 'cause here
she comes again."

"Oh God," I muttered, "here we go again."

I squeezed Dusty up to a trot and moved out along side of the bunch.
I couldn't believe my misfortune, 'cause here came that woman. I swore
to God; Dusty and I were just like a magnet. Her horse's nose was dang
near up Dusty's butt. I'd had enough; time to take the gloves off.

"Look lady," I snarled, "you have been on my horse's butt for the last
two days. We've got three more to go. Frankly, I'm dam tired of you
hanging on our tail. I've asked you politely, but you don't seem to get
it. So now I'm telling you stay the hell away from us. I'm warning you.
The next time you climb Dusty's tail, I'm just gonna let her kick the
crap out of your gelding. Got it!"

Several people nearby heard my rant and I swear they applauded.
Evidently, I wasn't the only person who had to put up with this lady's
poor trail etiquette. For her part, the woman jerked her horse around,
left in a huff, and hopefully, found someplace else to roost. I was hoping
this would be the end of this affair.

The next day brought a little excitement. Besides the temperature
heating up, so did the events of the day. We were riding through an
area of heavy timber and brush. This was privately owned land and
the rancher ran cattle and horses out on open pastures. He decided
he'd let the cattle be, but would bring in his horses. Cattle would

be less likely to stampede through a bunch of trail riders strung out for a mile or better, but horses . . . wouldn't put it past them, just 'cause. Evidently, he didn't get them all rounded up 'cause long about mid-afternoon we heard some crashing and pounding through the brush. Some folks surmised the noise was caused by deer or elk, but I reasoned not this time of year. They'd more than likely be up in higher elevations; I figured the thunder was caused by lively livestock. Sure enough through the brush came three twelve-hundred-pound horses right through the middle of a group of riders. Things got western for a little bit. Obviously, pampered show horses don't know anything about half wild ranch horses that have been left out on pasture for a year or two. Several of those western pleasure horses went to crowhoppin'. They never really bucked . . . I'm not sure they knew how. Anyhow, a couple of ranchers in our bunch herded them off to a safe distance from our merry group. I swear those three horses were literally horse laughing.

OUR RIDE WAS coming to an end and it was a good thing too. The heat index kept rising . . . for the week the mercury was hovering between 104 to 107. As things turned out, that particular stretch in July was the hottest on record; naturally the heat wave happened to coincide with the Asotin County Fair 50th Anniversary Trail Ride. The heat was taking a toll on not just the horses but riders also. Three people had to drop out because of heat stroke. I had never been bothered by the heat until a couple years later, then I had a severe heat stroke. I've never been able to tolerate heat since . . . twenty-three years in fact. I know that it's nothing to mess with . . . seems like you're never going to cool off. A couple of those show horses didn't fare any better. Two horses in particular were hit hard. One was so dehydrated the vet had to pump thirty-five gallons of fluid in him and the fool owner rode him the next day—unbelievable. The other horse was more fortunate; he only required five gallons of fluid and the owner loaded him up and took him home. Everyone urged the former to take his horse home, but he adamantly refused.

"I paid for this ride and I'm going to finish it," he said.

I guess you can't fix stupid. Fortunately for the horse, the last part of the ride was across relatively flat, open rangeland. At least the poor horse wouldn't have to work too hard. Dusty wasn't immune to some pain of her own. Remember when I mentioned I bought a different saddle? Guess what. The saddle sored her up. She wasn't striding out as she usually did, and when I unsaddled her I found out why. She had some sores on either side of her withers starting to form. I had the vet check her, and we made a rocker of sorts. First I slathered her withers up with Nitrofurazone, a florescent yellow antibiotic ointment used on livestock for cuts and abrasions. On top of the ointment, we folded up a thick towel in thirds and then the saddle pad on top. The ointment would provide protection of less friction. The vet figured that the eight-hour days of up and down caused the problem, whereas our rides to get into shape were of less duration and a day's rest in between. That's why the saddle didn't show signs of ill fit. I felt awful, but at least we were nearing the end. I can only assume that Dusty must have been in some discomfort, but she was so stoic you'd never know. (When we got home, I had to lay her up for three weeks before the sores, after the skin sloughed off, would heal.) I attributed her discomfort for the next event. 'Member the lady? She reappeared.

We were riding out in open country so folks, tired of riding single file spread out into smaller groups to enjoy conversation and camaraderie. There were people behind groups, but everyone gave each other plenty of room—with one exception. Sure as the day is long, miss lack of etiquette rode right up behind Dusty. Frankly, she was so busy yakking, I don't think she had any idea where she was in terms of proximity of other horses. Suffice to say, both Dusty and I had had enough.

"Okay Dusty," I whispered, "let fly."

Just that quick, Dusty's right hind foot flew back in one swift, smooth motion. Her ears were flat back and her aim was deadly. Her hoof contacted miss idiot's gelding's chest with a sickening thud. The gelding stopped dead in his tracks. I kinda felt sorry for the horse except that he was ill mannered in general, probably because he had an idiot owner who let him get away with murder. If truth be told, the way she acted around him, I'd say she was half afraid of him. Of course, the woman was outraged.

"You let your horse kick mine," she shouted. "Can't you handle your horse? You shouldn't be allowed on a ride like this with a horse that kicks."

Wouldn't you know that would be her reaction? I was trying to control my temper as best I could.

"Lady," I declared. "Don't pretend to condemn me or my horse, when, as far as I can tell, you don't know the first thing about trail etiquette. In the first place, your horse is ill mannered and in the second place, you clearly don't know to keep at least one-horse length between you and the rider in front. And lastly, you have been a literal pain in the butt for this entire trip. Your horse is dam lucky Dusty hit his breast collar and not hide. So get out of my face."

She turned her horse around and left thoroughly offended. I found out later she had been kicked out of the Lewiston saddle club for riding up on horses during horse shows. So there ya are.

We arrived at the rodeo grounds around three in the afternoon. The next day, Saturday, we were to ride in the parade. Given the circumstances: Dusty being sore and my disposition what it was, and the temperature just slightly cooler than hell, I decided not to ride in the parade. When I found Ben and Beth, I was ready to head for the barn.

"You look like something the cat dragged in," Ben sniggered.

I slid off Dusty and had to stomp my feet to get the blood running again. I started to unsaddle my pony.

"Here let me get that," Ben said.

Beth came around the trailer with a cold beer.

"Here have a seat. This should help." She smiled.

"Thank you," I breathed. "This will hit the spot . . . hope you have more than one."

As soon as Ben had the saddle off Dusty, the extent of her sore back became obvious.

"Dang, Terrie!" Ben exclaimed. "How did this happen?"

"Yeah, I know," I mumbled. "The vet and I thought she'd be okay to ride the last day. She didn't show signs of sorin' up until Thursday morning. I feel really bad. I have some bute in my gear. I'll give her another dose now. I guess when the hair grows back, my Appy will finally have a couple of white spots."

Once Dusty was taken care of, the three of us sat down for a cold one, or two, and talked about the trip. I asked about Red and of course, once he was home, he was fine. Strange how each horse is such an individual. Dusty could care less where she was as long as she got feed. Ben asked the obvious question.

"So are you planning to ride in the parade?"

I looked at him and my expression must have answered him.

" . . . I guess not." He smiled.

"Oh hell no!" I screeched. "I'm for heading home to a shower, soft bed, and air conditioning."

And with that decree we loaded Dusty and the gear and headed for home.

# Epilogue

Ninety-nine percent of this story is true. The only thing different is that I changed the names of my friend and her husband, primarily because we had a falling out soon after this ride. I feel confident she will never read this, still I'm not leaving anything to chance. As far as the description of the ride and the events as they occurred, all is true. My dear friend Cecil Hill's forewarning was spot on and stays with me to this day. I can scratch a long distance "social" trail ride off my bucket list. I was always curious about these rides, but I'm curious no more and I have no desire to do this ever again. I recall one rider's question. (He trailered his Arabian mare all the way from Seattle for this ride.)

"How are you enjoying the ride?" he asked

"I'd be having a lot more fun if there were a hundred and thirty-four fewer people along," I replied.

# PART IV

## MY FRIEND CAROLINE

When I was just a little jerk
My mom got hurt and couldn't do
All the things that needed work
A brand new trainer joined our crew.

TK said she went by Caroline
I'd seen her here a workin' Leif
She worked a lot with all equines
She made sure we all was safe.

TK liked her cause she said
"Caroline works ponies like me."
"A new adventure lies ahead.
She'll do ya good; wait and see."

Sure 'nough I went to work
Sometimes I tried her good
Try as I may I couldn't shirk
All my antics she withstood.

I'd start a circle to the left
Then as hard as I could
I'd fly off to the right
Man I fixed her really good.

'Cept Caroline was really smart
Next time I tried my little trick
Her trainin' skills--they was an art
My plan' she stopped perty darn quick.

When I was ready to do my flip
I got me the right amount of line
Slowly, so slowly the rope did slip
Her reactions quick, shook my spine

She best be ready; the game is on
Next time around I'll fix her hide
I'd turn so hard; I'd use brawn
Agin her brain and leave her bug-eyed.

She was strong; she matched my strength
She kept me movin'; I was plumb done in
Sore from stem to stern and so at length
She had me cold, I knew I couldn't win.

As time went on we built a bond
She taught me lots of things I'd need
When TK came back I'd really respond
That'll make Caroline proud indeed.

As much as I like friend Caroline
My mom TK could ne'r be replaced
When all healed up that mom of mine
Would take over trainin' I'll embrace.

Caroline took off my rebellious edge
I know my mom would still be sore
She don't want no torn cartilage
'Nother surgery she would abhor.

With TK back nothin' much changed
My ma (Dazz) was right when she told me
TK and Caroline are sure deranged
Come time for trainin' they both agreed.

I have to say with TK and me
For folks who may not understand
There's those who might disagree
'Cause she don't choose to reprimand

Mom's firm in all the things she does
Can't get away with nothin' much
I'm expected to behave and plus
When I'm good she's a real soft touch

'Sides yellin' makes our noggins throb
Don't do no good to yell and scream
Or use force and anger to do the job
That sure ain't in her overall scheme

In the end, one thing's for sure
I made a friend in Caroline
She comes back to reassure
We'll be friends for all time.

# Not Sixteen Hands!

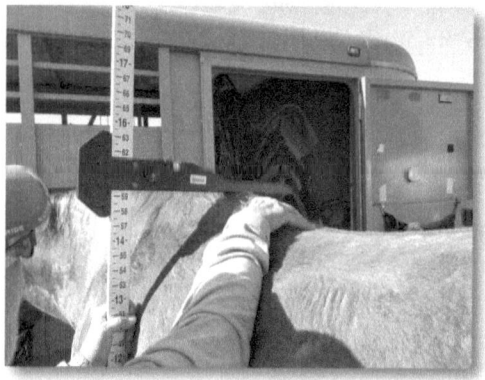

"I thought we had a deal," I said.
"No more than 15h," I said.
"I wouldn't need a crane," I said.
"To climb aboard yer back."

Here you are at twenty-one months
Ya stand at fifteen hands; I know
Yer sure to grow some more
Before yer three years old

I prize honesty above all else
In folks I call my friends
Horses don't get free rides
I require the same from them.

I had a horse a good while back
He cheated me but good.
He'd try and run me through a fence
He'd quit when work got tough

He'd buck and kick and whirl around
He'd sull up tight, not move an inch
He'd grump and grouse and groan
And his mouth was hard as stone

A fool made him hard to cinch
At the tiniest of pressure,
He'd puff up like a toad
Or pull back like a fool

Let me tell you one thing true
I tried ev'r thin' I knew to do
My patience wore down so low
There was nothin' left to give

Finally I had to give him up;
Which dang sure ain't my nature
Ol' Paint and I was sure to clash
At every twist and turn

He's livin' on another ranch
And last I heard his doin' well
That ol' boy don't ask too much
Ol Paint likes that just fine.

I s'pose yer wonderin'
What's Ol' Paint to you
I'll make this plain as day
Be honest as the day is long

Don't ever make me sorry
I bred your mamma Dazz
Be good to me; I'll be good to you
And don't grow past fifteen hands.

# ONE OF THOSE DAYS

Ol' Sol is up; the air is crisp.
I'm ready to start my day.

Hot coffee revs me up.
I'm out the door by eight.

My colt needs more work
Off I go a headin' for the barn.

The drive ain't bad at least for now
Construction's almost done.

At least there ain't new home tracts yet
There's still pasture wide and green.

The vet greets me at the barn,
Thank God she ain't here for me

I've had enough a payin' vets
My horses are hale and hardy.

Speakin' of which I went to find
Gus outstanding in his pasture

He's made good friends and I'll be danged
If he ain't found a new adopted daddy!

Danny's happy he's got a new colt to raise.
Gus can't figure why this daddy ain't got spots.

And he's wondrin' why his mamma looks like Danny.
But I know for sure he's Appy through and through.

Karma bein' what it is my day was 'bout to turn.
'Cause Gus was clean across the pasture.

Ya know a horse would rather eat than run around in circles.
He saw the halter in my hand and stood there swattin' flies.

"Gus c'mere," I called in vain. He stood as still as death.
"S'pose I'll have to walk out there to get yer ornery hide."

It weren't no problem to fit the halter on his head.
Then he put his nose right in my chest searchin' for his candy.

"Oh no you don't," I sternly said. "You made me walk out here!
If you think you earned a treat, you best be thinkin' some more."

Now that I had him haltered up, I turned to walk away.
He followed 'long right next to me just like he always did.

We hadn't gone not fifteen steps
My pretty day went south.

I felt a hoof just graze my toe
But friends that's all it took.

Next thing I knew, I was on my butt
And Gus was lookin' down at me.

Human nature is truly such
I looked around you see.

If someone saw my frivolity.
No, thank goodness praise the Lord

My pride was broke, but not no bones
How do I to get off this gall dam ground

I rolled on over and sat up straight
And assessed my current state.

'Member when I felt assured
No one saw me tumble down?

Well that ain't strictly true
For reasons I ain't figured yet

Four sets of eyes were trained on me
Wonderin' what the hell's she doin'.

The stallion and his two boys you see
Had walked on up to have a look at me

They watched me close; they didn't move
They was sure as hell transfixed.

I shook my head; I knew dang well
Down deep inside they laughed at me

I wallered to my hands and knees
When a simple thought come up.

I'll get a foot up under me
And heave myself upright

With a grunt and a groan up I came
I was standing straight and tall.
I brushed me off and grabbed my colt
Then proceeded toward the gate.

I looked at Gus and told him true
"If one word of this you breathe,

You'll find yourself away from me
Alive and well on another farm."

# THE ADJUSTMENT

"Why do we gotta move?" I whined.
"I like it here with all my friends," I moaned.
"'Cause TK says it's so," my mamma said.
"I'll bet TK pissed 'em off," I replied.

That was it one day in March
Don't know what the hell we're doin'
No way of knowin' who's in charge
'Cause most my life I spent in heaven.

Least momma would come with me
She always said TK would protect us
Ma said, "We trust TK don't we?"
"Life's an adventure! C'mom Gus."

Our adventure started out real bad
I refused to load up like I should
'Cause leavin' here sure made me sad
I wondered why Ma quietly stood.

Then she stomped her foot
I thought a bomb had blown
Loadin' up quickly sure went ca'put
Out I came like a bird that's flown

Weren't real dang smart on my part
'Cause I banged up my shoulder
Why I shoulda got a Purple Heart
A trailer's hard as a river boulder.

TK decided we needed help
One at a time alone she'd haul
I would cry with every step
I'd be here alone to bawl.

I shoulda known cause in a while
TK came back; she shook her head
"This here's Larry," I love that smile.
"Don't know why you felt misled."

I guess I wasn't so dang tough.
I loaded up so nice and calm
My leg was painin' me enough
And off we went to find my mom.

Ma was in a bright clean stall
There's lots of room to roll around
I sure was glad when I heard her call
In the paddock I could settle down

There's lots of comin's and goin's here
But we didn't have a pasture green
Our digs were nice but a bit austere
Ma it seemed weren't too dang keen

Up and down the fence she'd pace
I couldn't see why she should fear
We were together face to face
And I was thinkin' I liked it here.

TK taught me early on
"Don't be scared; nothin's wrong."
Ma was a different sort you see
If somethin' blew; man she'd snort.

I went to trainin' but I'd get sore
Somethin' got busted gettin' me here
The vet came round just to make sure
"It's soft tissue that's causin' hurt."

TK said, "Gus, no work for you."
Which was fine with me don't you see
I'd much rather watch the goin's on
'Cause I wasn't runnin' no marathon.

Since my leg wasn't healed
I lived in the hospital pen.
Ma lived with the old mares
It took a while but she got set

Months went by; I grew strong
TK decided it was time
To move out where I belong
I needed to see a different clime.
I'm in the pasture with the boys
I'm learnin' how to be a horse
And way out there ain't no noise
The things I learned are reinforced

There is one thing that makes me sad
I don't see mamma much anymore
We got separated and I should be mad
There ain't no point in causin' no uproar

That's the way the Creator plans
To help His children grow and learn
To be on our own in our lifespan
For a while our mother's love we earn.

I've adjusted well; I'm on my own
Straight and tall I'm a standin'.
I stiffened up my backbone
But I ain't been abandoned

I see my mamma ever now and agin
Things have change 'tween her and me
She likes me I know and she says hello
When we're apart I don't cry no more

I got my moms who take care of me
I see TK most; we got workin' to do
Claudia's a hoot; she thinks I'm a baby
She brushes, she pets; I get candy to chew.

When all's said and done, I sure like it here
Danny's a stud, but he's taken me in
Left the old place without sheddin' a tear
One thing's for sure I won't go back again'.

# THE SCRATCHIN' POST

I've raised a good horse or two
From a youngins' to full grown
When I'd start deep down I knew
I didn't want no clone.

Then I'd fix mistakes I made
I'd not do the things I done
That might make me afraid
So with my colt I'd have fun.

The most irritatin' vice you see
Is when them colts are young
I need to have them trust in me
They need to know they're safe.

I like to rub and scrub them clean
'Cause babies sure get grimy
Groomin' gives their coat a sheen
And 'sides they won't get flighty.

But one thing I'll make darn sure
I'll be damned if I turn out to be
My last mistake will not recur
I give fair warnin' dothca see

No one workin' with my colt
Will not go near its hind end
And if they do they'll get a jolt
Clear across the barn I'll send

To the poor unsuspectin' soul
Pray to the father, son and holy ghost
That they give you more self control
You'll become what you hate most.

'Cause I been down that road before
They was cute when they rubbed
Their little rump we all adored
They was small so no one cared.

I'll tell you true I did rethink
Twelve hundred pounds aimed at my ribs
Gave me pause 'cause in a blink
I got tossed in the darn hay crib.

My big ol horse weren't bein' mean
She was doin' what she always done
Since she was a foal plumb grass green
Just askin' for a scratchin' on her rump.

My advice please take to heart
Afore that baby begins to boast
They got you from the very start
And you've become a scratchin' post.

# PART V

# BEFORE THE BEGINNING

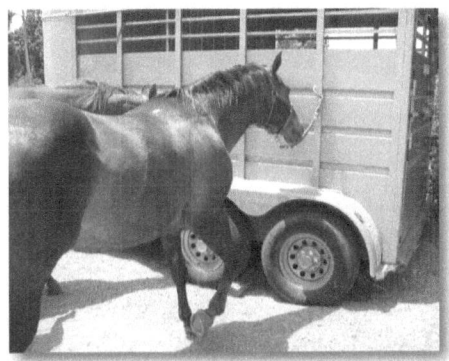

JANUARY 29, 2015 was a day no different than any other. I had my lessons prepared and my students were ready to learn whatever I wished to impart . . . not. No, really my students were pretty darn good. I was pleased with their progress and I didn't have any terrible discipline issues. English 10 honors and juniors and seniors. Now nearly three years removed from that date, I can't remember what unit we were working on, but for the purposes of this story that doesn't matter. The phone call I received shook me to the core . . . that's trite and overused . . . but what the hell.

I had barely gotten my students ready to go when my cell rang. I was very adamant that there would be no cell use in my classes . . . "put your phones away or they're mine . . ." I told my kids. That rule applied to me as well. So they knew if my cell rang there was something very serious going on. I apologized to my first period class and said hello.

"Terrie, there is something seriously wrong with Dusty. She's sopping wet and keeps wanting to roll. I think you'd better get out here," the voice said.

"Alright, I'll be right there," I replied.

Dusty was critically ill. I was soon to hear the one word a horse owner never wants to hear . . . cholic. I've seen horses with acute cholic, but fortunately my horses have never had bouts of cholic. Dusty, she was as strong as, well, a horse. She had been injured seriously, but she had never been sick. When she was injured, she wasn't a baby; she was stoic. She was a good patient; she always knew somehow, I would do whatever was necessary to make her better. But what was about to happen, I couldn't make better.

I called the front office and requested someone cover my classes and they'd better be quick because I was going to leave covered or not. Everyone at school, students, staff, and admin alike knew my animals were not like my children, they were my children. I had a friend back home (in Idaho) who never called me to look after their children; I guess they knew I wouldn't be up for that, but they knew I'd drop everything to look after their animals.

During the twenty-minute drive, I tried to keep my head on my shoulders and my brain from going into overload, but nothing prepared me for what I saw. By the time I got to the barn, UC Davis Veterinary Field Service was already there.

Dusty was in extreme distress. She was obviously in a good deal of pain, and I knew this wasn't just a simple case of cholic; she had twisted a gut. Understand, horses have seventy-two feet of intestines "crammed" into their body cavity and they aren't attached . . . they just sort of float around. If a horse gets down and starts thrashing around or rolling over and over (to alleviate pain) their intestine can twist . . . just like a kink in a hose. If the blood supply is cut off for very long, that section of intestine dies, everything backs up and there you go . . . the situation was bleak at best.

The field service vets performed a rectal exam . . . her feces was dry; not a good sign. They dosed her with a large amount of oil in an effort to get things moving, but to no avail. Nothing was moving. She was exhausted because in addition to the pain, the folks at the barn kept walking her to keep her from rolling so she would exacerbate and already critical condition. They had also given a large amount of pain killer to make her more comfortable; they then helped me load her into the trailer for the twenty-minute ride to Davis.

I must say, everyone involved in Dusty's care were great. There was a level of caring most human hospitals never show, but should. As for Dusty, she was as stoic as ever and she continued to suck on her lead rope like she always did, which made for a sloppy lead rope, but I always let her get away with sucking and chewing on her "pacifier." The doctors did a belly tap with ominous results. There was blood in the fluid which was not a good sign. They rushed her to surgery. I wanted the doctors to do what they could, but above all, Dusty was not to suffer. We agreed that halfway through the surgery, they would come out and let me know what they found.

My heart broke with the news. Let's just say, "it weren't good." There wasn't enough live tissue to reconnect her intestine. They could try, but at her age (twenty-five) even though she was in otherwise good health, the prognosis wasn't good and she could have recurring issues. I said no. Don't revive her, let her go in peace. The doctors let me go in to say goodbye . . .

WELL NOW. THAT was a long way around the bush to get me to where I wanted to be and I have to say I've never put any of this on paper before. Even though I'm almost three years removed from Dusty's passing, the pain (of her loss) is just as great. I miss her presence for sure. I still have the memories of the twenty-five years she was on this earth with me. This will sound backassward, but what I miss most is what we were going to do together for the next ten years. I was confident she was going to live to a ripe old age into her thirties; she was that healthy. But I'm getting ahead of myself.

Dazz was bred . . . I mean really bred. She had just a month or so to go before she foaled. Dazz and Dusty had a history; they were buddies; they lived together from the time Dazz was a long yearling. They were stalled next to each other, then pastured next to each other, but oddly enough they weren't herd bound. There are folks who believe animals don't grieve, but they are clearly ignorant; animals do grieve, especially herd animals. Granted, they don't grieve as long as humans do, but then humans always make such a big production out of everything. Suffice to say, Dazz knew the pasture next door was empty; Dusty wasn't there. She had no way of knowing Dusty wouldn't be returning . . . not bodily anyway.

Okay, I have left you all hanging long enough. This is the meat of the story. Dusty was an Appaloosa, the horses of the Nimiipuu. The Nez Perce Indians called the Pacific Northwest home. Specifically, they lived in the land known as "the Palouse." This region today encompasses north central Washington and Idaho. Their lands also ranged from the Wallowa country in northeast Oregon and southeast Washington to the Snake and Clearwater regions of central Idaho. They raised the Appaloosa to be a small, sturdy mount, very much like a mustang, that could travel through the very wild and rough country in which they lived. The characteristic spotted coat patterns weren't purely for show. The variety of coat patterns served as camouflage that gave the Nez Perce an advantage when hunting or in battle.

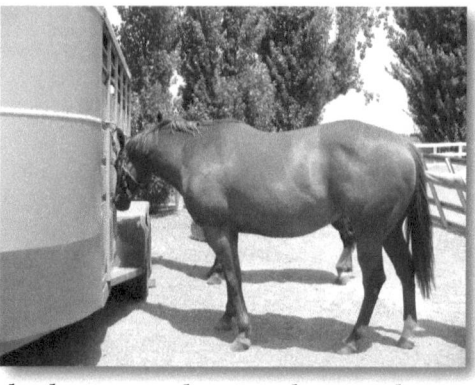

Naturally, Dusty, I'm sure for spite, never colored. She was a solid liver chestnut, but still Appaloosa through and through. As such, when she died, she deserved a traditional (as close as I could make) Native ceremony whereby her ashes would be thrown to the four winds and her spirit could return to the Creator, while her body returned to Mother Earth. So, that's what I did.

I brought her saddle, pad, and bridle into her pasture along with her pasture buddy. I draped a replica blanket that Chief Joseph wore over Dazz's back. I was more than a little surprised at Dazz's behavior. She is known to be a little fractious, but all through the ceremony, she stood stock still. I believe she felt Dusty's presence . . . we all did. I asked several of our friends to join Claudia and me during the ceremony. Without getting into every detail, suffice to say I said a prayer in the Nez Perce language and cast Dusty's ashes to the four winds. At the end, I made a paste of her ashes and drew a line across both Dazz's forehead and mine, then we touch our heads together. This was so weird because Dazz never moved a millimeter. We stayed together, for some seconds, to allow Dusty's spirit flow through and into us forever. I can't remember a time in my life I experienced anything that spiritually powerful. My friends said later they felt something happening as well. Now, I'm sure to many of you, this may sound a little silly and even crazy, but Native American spiritualism is real; their beliefs are real; and no one will ever convince me to discount them as fiction or myth.

Finally, I have arrived at "before the beginning," bet you're glad too, huh. Once again, I'm going to relate events that, to some of you, will be explained away as simply coincidence. Go ahead, but I'm sorry, knowing Dusty the way I did, no one can make me believe these events are mere coincidence. When Gus finally arrived, and I began the process of getting to know him, I noticed subtle nuances in his character, that reminded me of Dusty. At first, I, like many of you, figured I was seeing what I wanted to see, except these nuances became full blown character traits that were just like Dusty. These are a few examples: facial expressions, the way he carried himself, the way he approached us, and finally, the last strongest piece of evidence. Whenever he was going to do something he wasn't supposed to do, he would walk far enough away that I couldn't reach him (to stop him), he would turn and look at me to make sure I was watching. I swear, before you reach the conclusion I should be committed, I could see Dusty looking through Gus at me, laughing. Now lest you think these are the ravings of a crazy old woman, everyone who interacted with Dusty over the years said the same thing. In many ways, Dusty has been reincarnated in Gus.

What I'm really going to miss is what I would have done with Dusty. She was going to be my training partner. Since she was not his mother, I could put them together, wean him away from Dazz, and not have to worry about him trying to nurse . . . at least after the first try. Dusty was going to provide what I couldn't, equine education. She would teach Gus how to behave in a herd of two. She would be dominant, just like I was going to be in our herd of two. I was going to be able to pony Gus off of Dusty. She was pretty darn good out on the trails . . . Dazz tended to spook, but a body never knew exactly what would set her off or when. I've had several broken ribs and a collar bone to prove that. Dusty was going to be a surrogate mother. But then what was it the Bard said long ago? Something about "the affairs of mice and men . . ."

Dusty has been gone for nearly three years now, but I firmly believe that with Gus around, she really isn't gone at all. The more I work with Gus, the more my beliefs are confirmed. He accepts being handled, usually, pretty well. He picks up the different elements and levels of training in stride. And he's smart. Of course, many young horses will behave in much the same way, but with Gus and Dusty the similarities between the two are manifested in their characters. I'm sure many of you can't accept what I have described on face value. I suppose you would have had to been around both horses to believe my tale. I tell you there is a spiritual aspect to all of this and I will take my beliefs to my grave.

FOR NOW, GUS'S story has come to an end. He's coming three and will soon be taught everything he needs to know to become a trusted mount and partner. Of course, his education will be ongoing. I believe that a horse's training never ends. Every time you come in contact with a horse you are teaching him something . . . for good or ill. Suffice to say, I hope I am teaching Gus the former not the latter.

Gus has always been and will continue to be curious and willing. His laidback nature can be a blessing and a curse. Generally, a laidback horse isn't spooky; although there are times a horse will spook at his own shadow. Gus has taken everything I've done with him in stride and I'm relatively sure he will continue to do so. That's the blessing part. The curse comes in because he is so laidback he tends (on occasion" to be lazy. "I just don't want to work today, mom" is his mantra. What do I do then, continue to encourage, firmly, not abusively. And what do you know, like a recalcitrant child, he gives in and does what I ask.

All of the horses I've owned were raised and trained for mountainous travel. We traversed up and down canyons in central Idaho and southeastern Washington. My horses learned to be sure footed, tough, brave, and reliable. They would go in any direction I pointed them. Many places were "steep as a cow's face," but away we went and always returned home safely. I'd just give 'em their head and let them take the lead. Gus, on the other hand, has been raised, so far, in flat land country. He hasn't seen much but traffic and canal roads. And, I imagine that will continue in as much as he's come along later in my life. I doubt I'll be going up into the mountains or other rough country. And, ya know what, that's okay.

After the initial euphoria of breeding Dazz had passed, I had to decide what I would do with the resulting foal. Since I lost Dusty, I decided I wanted a good reliable trail horse. I wanted a horse I didn't need to work hard to keep physically and mentally in shape. Some horses have to be longed every day to take the edge off . . . hum, Dazz comes to mind here. I wanted a horse just like Gus. Well, what do you know about that?

I don't know what the future holds for Gus and me. Will he become the next great reining champion? That would be nice. Will he be a cutter? A reined cow horse? So far I'm building the foundation for all of these things. Some folks say Gus won't reach his full potential being a pleasure horse . . . no not Western Pleasure (OMG! Don't get me started). To those I say, "So what!"

One thing I know for sure whatever we decide to do, we'll do it together and we'll have fun. And when it comes right down to it, isn't that why we own horses in the first place?

"HELLO," I MUTTERED.

"We have a foal on the ground," the voice said.

Suddenly I was wide awake.

"Okay, we'll be right out, thanks," I replied.

"Claudia!" I shouted. "Dazz had her baby. C'mon, let's go."

The boarding facility is in Vacaville, and we live in Fairfield. Claudia planned to go to work, (not me) so she took her car. I must have driven out there and back thousands of times in the last ten years, but this time, do you think I could have found my way? Hell no! I swear to God I got lost. Maybe because I was half asleep or because it was dark. Hell if I know, but I drove right past the entrance before I figured out where the hell I was. Needless to say everyone got a chuckle at my expense over that.

"We saw your car go by, where were you going?" Claudia asked.

"Beats me. I got lost, I guess," I said sheepishly. "Evidently, I haven't had enough coffee. Where are they?"

"Clear at the end of the pasture," Claudia said.

"Have you gone out to look?" I asked.

"No, we were waiting for you."

Jan had a high-powered flashlight, so I shined it out in the direction I figured Dazz had taken her foal. Fortunately, Jan came out of the house with coffee.

"Oh, thank you." I sighed. "This should do the trick."

Not only did I need the caffeine to wake me up, it was dang cold. Yeah, I know this is California, not Idaho, but I have gotten soft in my old age.

"Are you coming?" I said to Claudia.

"Yes! I'm right behind you."

I decided I'd better remind Claudia the baby probably wouldn't have color.

"Now ya know this baby probably won't have spots," I cautioned.

I could feel hot eyes boring into my back.

"I just don't want you to get your hopes up, that's all."

I walked as quietly as I could, given the fact I couldn't see where to put my feet; even with the flashlight I was tripping and stumbling around. Once we got close enough to see, I knew I was going to have to eat crow.

"Well, I'll be dammed . . . he's got spots. I never would have thunked it." I laughed.

"I told you he'd have spots," Claudia exclaimed. "Now, is the foal a filly or a colt?"

"I don't know, let me look." I wanted a filly, not a colt.

Fillies, in my experience were just easier to train. There was no science behind my belief, I just wanted a filly. I didn't want to mess with a gelding's plumping . . . cleaning a gelding's sheath wasn't my idea of fun.

"Near as I can tell, we have a filly, I think."

"Don't you know how to tell?" Claudia laughed.

"A course I do, but it's dark and she's got her but wedged next to the fence. And Dazz is no help. Get your butt out of my way, ya big boob. Yes, we have a filly. I guess we'd better call the vet and get her to check her out to make sure she's okay."

We'd been there about an hour and finally we had enough light to see. The baby had gotten up and was trying to figure out how to get some breakfast. Something should have told me I may have been in error regarding the sex of this little devil because it seemed like forever before he finally latched on to a teat and began nursing. Dazz, for her part, was doing her level best to be a good mom. She was a maiden mare and sometimes they aren't sure about what the heck is going on. Sometimes nature needs a little help, but obviously, and to my relief, Dazz was going to be a good mom.

I got the colt's navel stub doused good with Betadine solution and fortunately, we didn't have to put the baby through the indignity of an enema. Oftentimes, equine babies need a little help for that first bowel movement, but everything came out okay. So we just needed to wait for the vet to arrive to give the little bugger a couple of shots.

"So ya got your baby." The vet smiled. "What did you get, a filly or a colt?"

"A filly." I grinned. "So, how do you wanna do this?"

"You handle the mare and I'll look over the baby," the vet directed.

"Great," I drawled.

I tried to keep Dazz from doing a tap dance all over me while the vet was working. After a minute, she looked up and laughed.

"You looked to see what you got?" The vet was beside herself. "You have a colt."

"What?" I exclaimed.

"God, you guys. All you have to do is look for holes. A filly has two, a colt has one."

'Course Claudia and Jan weren't going to help me out.

"Hey, it wasn't us," Claudia said.

Oh yeah, great friends.

"What can I say? It was dark and I hadn't had enough coffee to wake up. Give me a break."

Both horses got their shots and the only thing left to do was check Dazz's placenta to make sure she expelled all of it. Mares can get a hell of an infection if any part of the placenta is left in her uterus. Upon inspection, we discovered something else. The placenta was all in one piece, but where it was located left us scratching our heads. We found it just outside the barn door. Clearly, Dazz was inside, nice and cozy; Gus Gus was dropped out in the cold.

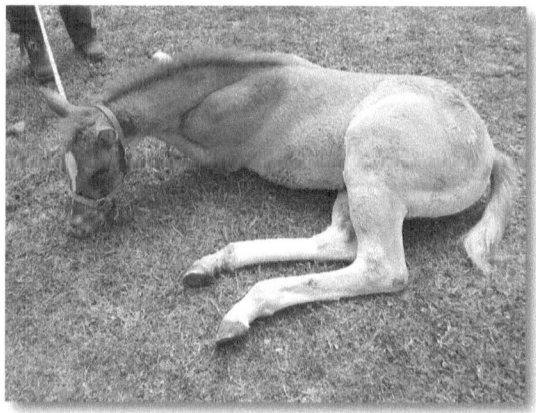

GUS WAS AND is pretty darn precocious. He's curious and brave. All of these qualities make for a good solid working horse; if they can be controlled. Too much of any one of these characteristics can prove harmful. Remember the old saw, "curiosity killed the cat." With that in mind, let me continue my tale.

Gus wasn't much more than two months old when he suffered a nasty cut on his inside right leg. Hide and skin was open to the bone from the top of the cannon bone all the way down to the long pastern bone. We still don't know how this happened. The foaling stall and the pasture were as safe as we could make them. The fences were good and stout "no climb" and the stall had no sharp protrusions anywhere. There was really only one plausible answer to his injury . . . his mamma.

For the cut to be that severe, and on the inside to boot, Dazz must have stepped on him and when Gus tried to free himself, Dazz scraped him from "stem to stern." So much so, that the injury required more than twenty-six stitches to close. The vet is remarkably talented. She had to use all of her considerable knowledge and experience to fix Gus Gus.

There were several things that made suturing Gus's wound tricky . . . the severity notwithstanding. First, the wound was several hours old when we found him. Second, in a very short period of time, the edges of the skin tend to shrink up leaving little viable tissue to cover the open wound, and lastly, and most dangerous for Gus would be sedating him. The wound would take some time to suture, even as quickly as the vet worked to close it. A colt as young as Gus could not be given a large enough dose (of anesthetic} to keep him unconscious for the duration (without harming him). We had to give him small doses repeatedly during the operation. Whenever he started to come awake, the vet would stop suturing and administer another dose of meds. This went on for better than an hour until she was done.

After the cut was sewn up, she bandaged up his leg and away he went soon after the drugs wore off. Then for every two to three days until his leg mended, we had to reapply a bandage. I have to say, I was amazed at how good he was about having his sore leg worked on. I wouldn't wish this on anyone who owns a young horse, but this experience certainly got Gus used to be handled. He got used to having the vet come and work on him as well. So, long story short, Gus recovered from his owie and the vet did such a wonderful suture job, there isn't much of a scar.

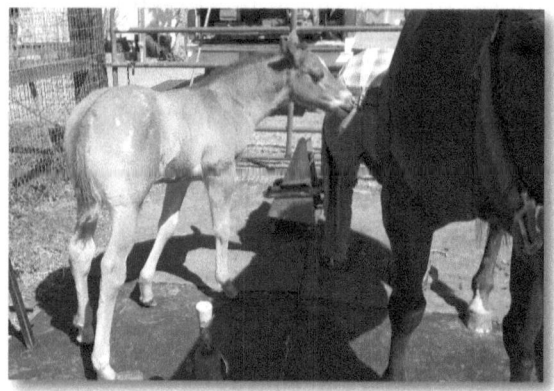

IF ONLY I had known Facebook folks would know everything I was doing with Gus, I might not have bred Dazz. Over the course of nearly three years, Gus has become a minor sensation. Thank God his goings on have been limited to Claudia's Facebook friends . . . and admittedly . . . mine as well. I had to get my foot in the door just to keep things on the up and up.

From the day Gus was foaled until present day, every time Gus so much as sneezed the folks on Facebook knew about. Photos and videos have been splattered on this social media platform. Everything from Gus's haltering lessons to his first sessions in the round pen for ground work. His lessons in lunging, long lines, his first saddling, and having a human laying over his back have all been documented.

When I decided he needed some time off for a few months, rather than fry his puny little brain, the hue and cry from his Facebook buddies was tumultuous to say the least. When I took a sabbatical from Facebook for as few months, people thought we'd both died. Now granted none of this went viral, understand, but Gus has had a large enough following that he was missed if we didn't post something every now and again.

So now we're getting close to Gus's third birthday (in February) and we will begin riding him in earnest. He will be big and strong enough to be ridden at least three times a week in thirty-minute sessions. He and I will start out slowly at first: most everything he will learn will be at the walk, then to the trot, and finally at the lope. He'll be able to turn over his hocks, back up, and move laterally off the slightest of pressure.

No bit or spurs to begin . . . a side pull and my legs will do the asking. He's been very good about learning things, so I'm not too worried that he'll pitch a fit, but then again, with a colt, you never know what goes on in their pea size brain, or what might set them off.

My advice to Gus's Facebook following is to stay tuned, there is more to come . . .

MY FATHER USED to say to me, "Terrie never jump into things. Think before you make any decision, but especially big decisions. You have to think about the future. Remember every decision you make will affect everyone around you, not just you." Yes indeed, words to live by . . . wished I'd have listened. You're probably wondering what this sage advice has to do with Gus and me. There's a better than even chance had I listened to my father's advice, I wouldn't have Gus. This is how things went down . . .

In March of 2014, I was in need of some horse "stuff" so I decided to go up to the tack store. This was a thirty-minute drive and I didn't favor going alone, so I asked my friend if she would like to ride along. She had nothing better to do so she said fine and off we went. The time went zipping by . . . talking about horse stuff and gossip and in no time arrived at our destination. We shopped for our horse supplies and visited with the clerks for a while and then headed for home.

In the foyer, there is a bookshelf wherein every free horse magazine known to exist resides. On the way out my friend picked up several . . . *Pacific Coast Cutting Association, Horsemen's Digest,* and others . . . mistake number one.

My friend leafed through magazine after magazine until she hit upon an Appaloosa stud named Totally Bedazzled RA

"Look here," she exclaimed, "this stallion has Dazz's name in it."

"Hey! I'm trying to drive. I can't be looking at magazines," I retorted. However, the seed had been planted . . . mistake number two.

Because a horse has the same name as my mare is not reason enough to breed her. Any ethical horse breeder will not encourage a mare owner to breed their mare just because names match. There is so much more to consider. For example, is the mare in breeding shape . . . that is, is she "reproductively" healthy? Are her estrous periods cycling correctly? Do both the mare and the stallion have the genetic make-up needed to produce the type of horse you want . . . i.e., cutting, reining, reined cow horse, etc. And of course disposition is another very important characteristic to consider. I sure didn't need another "Dizzy Dazz." Sure this horse was an Appy (what I wanted), he had color (what I wanted), and the breeding fee was reasonable. All these things were working against any kind of logic. Was I listening to my father's wisdom you ask? Well, his voice was in a kingdom far, far, away . . . mistake number three.

Okay, there you have it . . . three strikes against good decision making. Don't rush to judgment . . . don't make rash decisions.

Look before you leap. Breeding my mare would be like having a child . . . I'd be responsible for another life indefinitely. Also, there was the added expense of raising another horse. Shoot, I didn't even know if the boarding facility would have room for another horse. All I kept saying to myself was that there would be no harm in just looking. Oh yeah, I'd been down that road before. One long president's day weekend Claudia and I went "just looking" for a truck. We came home with a 1998 Ford Expedition. That impulse buy turned out really good, but I couldn't expect lightning to strike twice, could I?

I dropped my friend off at the barn and headed for home. I kept rolling this breeding deal over and over in my mind. The wise choice would be just to forget the whole thing. And I sure as hell shouldn't tell Claudia . . . I pretty much knew how that would turn out. Yeah, just forget the whole thing. We already had two horses; that was plenty. Just forget it. Now hold that thought . . .

I had barely walked through the front door when Claudia asked what I bought. I explained that I only bought what I went up there for . . . I didn't do any impulse buying . . . yet I thought. I couldn't believe the next words out of my mouth.

"How would you feel about breeding Dazz?" I asked. Dang! I was having an out of body experience. *You idiot I said to myself. What in the world are you doing?*

"We're going to have a baby," Claudia cooed. OMG. I'm screwed, I thought.

"Now wait just a minute. I'm thinking that's all." I was backwatering as fast as I could.

"There's an Appy stud I want to look at up in Clements," I cautioned. "All I want to do is look . . . nothing more."

"That's good. We'll have an adventure," Claudia exclaimed. OMG! I'm really screwed.

Gerardot Performance Horses in Clements, California was and is a big time Appaloosa ranch. Year in, year out they take horses to the National and World Championships and win. Their horses are put together well and have good minds as well. They have several stallions to choose from, but I wanted to see Totally Bedazzled RA. As it turned out, I wasn't sure Dazz and Totally Bedazzled RA would be a good match. Gerardot's trainer asked what discipline I had in mind for the resulting foal, and I told him reining or cutting. He showed me another stallion, Gossip Spotted Me . . . a red dun with frosting over his hips and all the Appaloosa characteristics . . . mottled skin, striped hooves, and the sclera showing. More important than color, he was put up well and had a good mind . . . just what I wanted. Oh hell.

Before I knew what was happening, I was filling out papers and writing a check. Dazz was gonna be a momma. All this from an advertisement in a "free" magazine. My friend and I were gonna have a serious talk when I got back. On the way home, Claudia and I discussed all the ins and outs of breeding a mare. The whole process is a little more complicated than one might think. You just don't throw the stallion and mare together and let nature take its course. There are all kinds of vet bills for ultrasounds, palpitating the mare, etc. Then there's mare care . . . keeping the mare happy and healthy for the two months she'd be at the breeders, and finally the breeding fee. In all actuality, there is less expense involved if ya go out and buy a colt. 'Course then ya don't have the fun of raising the thing from ground up. Oye.

I cautioned Claudia about some of the things that could go wrong . . .

"Now, I want you to understand this isn't a done deal," I said.

"What do you mean?" Claudia questioned. "Dazz is gonna have a baby."

"There is a chance she might not take and even if she does, she might slough the foal (miscarry). I just want you to be prepared, just in case," I warned.

"Okay," Claudia said. "Dazz is gonna have a baby."

"Then there is the matter of color," I cautioned. "Remember, Dazz is a quarter horse, solid colored. Chances are, she won't throw color."

"What?" Claudia was in a daze.

"The foal probably won't have spots," I declared.

"Dazz is gonna have a baby." I give up.

Well, long story short, Dazz was at the breeders for better than sixty days, but she settled, and we brought her home and impatiently waited for another forty-five days to have an ultrasound to make sure she was bred. The vet came out and sure enough the ultrasound bore out good news. Need I say anything?

"We're gonna have a baby!" Claudia exclaimed. "We're gonna have a baby!"


GETTING DAZZ BRED was the easy part of this deal. Next we had to decide on a name. Good thing the gestation period for a foal to be born is eleven months. I'm telling you, it took every bit of that time. What an ordeal!

"Why do we have to name the baby that way?" That was more of a demand than a question.

"Naming a foal is always done this way. Tradition my dear, tradition," I said.

"Well, it's stupid." She was more than a little wound up.

On the other hand, I was a little more than exasperated. How do you explain this kind of thing to a nonhorse person? Don't get me wrong, Claudia has learned a whole bunch about keeping and training horses in the last seventeen years. Still, she hasn't gone through breeding and then raising the resulting foal. While I have been around my own horses most of my life adult life, I have learned a really whole bunch about horses. How I work with horses has become second nature. I forget that I do things automatically without having to think about it and Claudia wants me to explain everything. I tend to lose my patience, then the fight's on. Which isn't her fault . . . most of the time.

"Registered horses have always been named this way. You take a name from the stud and one from the dam. That way when you go to sell them, people have a good idea the horse's line. Makes good sense to me," I explained.

"Well, it makes no sense to me," Claudia declared.

"Okay, let's do this." I sighed. "We'll each make a list of names for both a colt and a filly, then throw out the ones we don't like. Once the foal is born, and we know the sex, we have to send in three names (in case our first choice is already taken)."

I couldn't believe I was willing to compromise rather than arbitrarily choosing a name and been done with it.

"Alright," Claudia said, "that'll work."

OMG. The whole thing has been done for almost four years and I'm exhausted just writing about this. We must have had twenty names to sort through, but we finally settled upon Dazz's Lil Gossip. Gossip Spotted Me and Infinitely Bedazzled are his parents, thus the name. We called him Gus Gus (from Cinderella . . . the lil fat mouse whose shirt was too small. They called him Gus Gus.) His daddy's call name was Gus. There wasn't a very big leap to come up with that. But as he grew Gus Gus grew out of his name. Now he's simply Gus.

And grew he did, but I don't want to get ahead of myself . . .

To be honest, I hadn't bred a mare for twenty-six years and that baby was the only foal I'd raised to this point. But I have to say, that turned out really well. Ha Dar's Dusty Rose [a.k.a. Dusty] was probably the best horse I'd ever had. She lived to be twenty-five; sadly I had to put her down long before her time. Dazz was still carrying Gus when Dusty twisted a gut in a freak accident. But this is another story.

We waited, one of us more patiently than the other, for the next eleven months for Dazz to deliver. She was bred in March, so I knew she'd foal the end of February or the first week of March. In the middle of February, she started to show signs of the foals impending birth. She started to bag up, the muscles at the base of her tail commenced to soften. Claudia was going nuts . . . I was just waiting. Then on the evening of the twenty-third of February Dazz started dripping milk. I knew in the next twenty-four to thirty-six hours we'd have a baby on the ground. Sure enough at 4:30 a.m. February, 25, 2015, Dazz's Lil Gossip was on the ground.

# THE TERRIBLE TWOS

JUST LIKE HUMAN toddlers, colts go through a period where they are a little hard to control. They are into everything. Don't leave anything out, within reach, because that "thing" will be lost. And, if your colt is anything like mine, like a human toddler, the item goes right into the mouth.

Gus was (and is) a master at grabbing anything he isn't supposed to have. Case in point; I like to keep a hand towel in my back pocket: to wipe my brow, clean out horse eyes . . . any number of things for which I might need a towel. I should have known better considering the years I've spent working with and around horses and observing horse behavior. As an aside and by way of illustration, my Dusty Rose took everything she could get her teeth around: gloves, hammers, buckets, and (believe me or don't) post hole diggers. Off she would go, then drop whatever she had clear at the other end of a two-acre pasture. Gus evidently has inherited this trait . . . but that is another story. Just when my back was turned, Gus would grab the towel and off he would go. Sometimes he would flip the towel from side to side, throw the darn thing up in the air, stomp on it, then pick the towel up and eat the blasted thing. This is when a simple prank becomes dangerous. Whatever goes into a horse's mouth, if not spat out, has to go down his throat. At that point, I'd have a choking horse. Since a horse can't throw up, I had to get the towel out of his mouth, pronto. I at least learned my lesson and I keep the chewed-up towel as a reminder. I still keep a towel handy, securely tucked under my belt in front, not in my back pocket. "Some folks live and learn and some folks just live." Thanks dad.

I really try to keep my horses as comfortable as possible. Believe me when I say they are not pampered; they are large farm animals and they can hurt you. They have to be taught there are things they have to endure in order for them to be taken care of. The best way to teach a horse to learn stand patiently is grooming. As I said, I have been around horses most of my life. I've trained a number of horses and in my experience, they have all been pretty good about standing still, not tap dancing all over my toes, pulling back, or just being an all 'round pain in the butt. Well, then along came Gus. I swear, people might actually think Gus was taught to dance with his hind end. All I had to do was get out the fly spray. He would go back and forth until I got dizzy trying to work with his hind quarters. He stood stock still when I would back off; he'd turn his head to watch me and as soon as I would walk toward his hind end, the two step would begin again. If the whole process wasn't so maddening, a guy could get a laugh or two.

He learned getting brushed was a really pleasant procedure (especially under his belly). I must say, he was (and is) the most tactile horse I've ever owned. Every horse has "that spot" he loves to have scratched. That place where the ol' neck stretches and the nose goes out and they wiggle around in pure ecstasy. Gus didn't have one . . . every place you scratched, rubbed, or brushed he seemed to thoroughly enjoy . . . until I got out the dreaded fly spray, then the dancing would begin. Eventually, he gave up the dance routine and stands quietly. He finally learned a little fly spray was better than flies bugging him all day and night.

The funny thing about Gus is that the things you would think should / would be a problem weren't: he's never been spookie; he's not pushy; he's pretty much taken things in stride. Of course, the way he has been handle for the two and a half years he's been on this earth has made a huge difference in the way he behaves. Still, I will be glad when he turns three and no longer have to deal with the terrible twos.

# PART VI

I NEEDED A good dose of "home." I felt I was chasing my tail and not getting anywhere. I felt there was something missing . . . not in my life necessarily, but in me. There was a big hole right in the middle of me. I had lost my focus, but most importantly, I had lost my culture. Yes, that had to be the problem; I had lost the most important part of me, the place of my origins that made me who I was.

So, home I decided to go; I would visit the places of my ancestors. But to do that, I would have to have a good horse, one that could carry me through the rough, wild country of my birth. Check that need off . . . a good horse I had. Dazz's Lil Gossip, aka Gus, would carry me wherever I wanted to go. There weren't many places with country as rough as the Grande Ronde, the Salmon, the Columbia, the Snake, and the Clearwater River drainages. The country that extends from the Bitterroots in Montana (which encompasses the Lolo Trail) to the Blue Mountains in Oregon, Washington, and Idaho seemed to be calling my name. All of these places together made up the traditional homeland of the Nimi Poo. As rough as that country was, the worse part of my renewal would be the long drive, horse trailer and all, from California to Lewiston, Idaho.

I knew this journey would be the most taxing trip I'd made in many years . . . not just on my sixty-eight-year-old body, but Gus's young body as well. When I was a child, I spent many happy summer camping trips into the mountains with my dad, but that was many moons ago and I wasn't thirteen anymore. I had been working out and lost a gob of weight, but my lung capacity wasn't what it once was. I had to be able to move around at altitude if I was to make this trip a success. And, Gus would have to be able to carry me up into the mountains without getting winded. Even though he was in his prime at five, Gus hadn't been ridden much in the mountains. So, to remedy that, I started riding him around the hills close to home, then we made an excursion or two up to the Sierras to get him really legged up. By the end of June, I figured we were both ready. I'd lost more weight and Gus was really muscled up and raring to go.

I rounded up all the gear I would need . . . I made a list, then checked it twice . . . more than once. I would begin my quest in Lewiston, so if I remembered something I might have overlooked, I could always purchase said item(s) there. Lewiston isn't in the back woods; as a matter of fact, they're quite civilized there. Claudia made sure I had my cell phone, "in case of emergencies" . . . which wouldn't work in the mountains, but I humored her and took the dam thing along. She wondered how I would carry everything I would need. After all she surmised I couldn't carry everything on Gus.

"Not to worry," I explained. "I have a friend back home who will let me borrow his pack mule. He's been in the mountains plenty; he's broke to pack really well."

"That's great," she replied, "but Gus has never led anything, let alone a mule."

"He has so," I retorted. "The last time I went to the Sierras, we practiced doing that very thing. Heck, he's ready to go."

"Okay." Claudia sighed. "If you're sure. All I can say is good luck. And take lots a pictures."

"Hey," I lamented. "This is a spiritual renewal of sorts, not just a vacation. I'd planned to leave all the technology in the truck."

Uh oh, that was an oops.

"What if you get into trouble," Claudia cried. "You said you'd have your cell phone."

"Yes," I reassured. "There might be a chance of having the dang thing work if a satellite passes overhead."

"I'll probably get as far as Hermiston today, so I'll call you when I get set up."

"All right," my friend said. "I hope you find what you're looking for on this trip."

After a bit of reflection, I replied, "So do I."

Good old Claudia. She has been a good friend for the last eighteen plus years. When the best friend I ever had, Gayle, died . . . damned f_ _ _ing cancer . . . I retired from the university in Berserckly. I floundered around for a while. I traveled some, but I didn't know what I was going to do with the rest of my life. I started writing cowboy poetry; that's when I met Claudia. She had/has an up-and-coming publishing company, and she was interested in publishing my work. The rest as they say is history. I'm not going to get rich from my books, but I supplement my retirement. I'm far from destitute; I had made some good investments and was able to buy my ranch.

I HAD TO admit that when I arrived at my destination, I was a little more than regretful at having to leave my fancy truck and trailer with attached living quarters. Life had gotten pretty cushy and sleeping on the cold, hard ground, even with a cushion wasn't like sleeping on a Temperpedic mattress. Oh well, the things we do for peace of mind. Anyway, the miles flew by. As much as I hated traffic and congestion, out on the open road, there's nothing like a freeway. Driving through Nevada, a body could go eighty miles per and the miles fly by. My dog (Baily) put up with my singing to Dave Stamey tunes and Gus trailered like a trooper. He liked taking a break, though, and when he got too tired he'd start stomping. That was my cue to find a place for the night. This trip, which normally took one day and a night, took us two days and two nights. We stopped at Hermiston, Oregon the first night and Twin Falls, Idaho the second. We arrived in Lewiston, specifically Hells Gate Park, the evening of the second day.

Before we left Twin Falls, I took stock of everything we had and anything I might need and made a stop at a tack store and then once at the grocery store. I didn't want to have to unhook the trailer and leave Gus unattended. The Lewiston-Clarkston Valley hadn't changed all that much in the intervening eighteen years I'd been gone. There were a few more fast food restaurants and other stores, but for the most part the old place hadn't changed. I got Gus's portable paddock set up, unloaded him, fed him, and he was settled in for the night. Now it was my turn. The valley is known to be hot as blue blazes in the summer, but the first of June was still pretty nice. The evenings were calm and cool and not too buggy. I hadn't been to Hell's Gate Park for years . . . there was about 165 acres designated for horse related activities and surprisingly enough, that hadn't changed. I figured what the heck; tomorrow I get ol' Gus saddled up and we go for a little ride.

After traveling eleven hundred miles, he needed to get a little exercise ... kinda stretch the muscles ... mine too.

Considering we began our journey during the workweek, there weren't a whole lot of people riding on the trails. That was fine with me; I'd just as soon not have to fight a bunch of people just to go down the trail. On the weekend there were people on top of people. I chose one particular trail I used to ride because it was rocky, narrow, and there was a creek to cross. Once you got up on top, the view was worth the ride. You could see up and down the Snake for miles. Straight across the river you could see Asotin, Washington. I loved riding up here. The view was and is incredible; thank God it hadn't changed. I tried to imagine a time when the river and the land had not been changed by white settlers and "progress" hadn't changed the river's course. Ah well.

I thought about visiting some friends and family before I headed up river, but I decided the heck with that. I had a long drive ahead of me and I had to stop in Kamiah to pick up Henry's pack mule ... Charley. Next morning I'd stow away the gear and Gus, Baily, and I would head out to arrive at the trail head on the Selway River, a four-hour drive.

Henry's place was across the Clearwater River a few miles above the Heart of the Monster, a Nez Perce holy place that the people believed to be where Coyote defeated the Monster of the Clearwater, and created the Nez Perce people. Henry was Nez Perce and had lived along the Clearwater all his life. He was my age, but still ran a pack string for tourists who wanted to see the back country. (He used to guide hunters, but got tired of how they disrespected the animals they hunted and Mother Earth which provided the game.) During the winter, Henry sculpted western art, made silver spurs and bits, and rawhide hackamores with horse hair mecates.

Charley was one of Henry's best pack mules. He was often the lead mule in the string and took care of the hole shooting match ... including Henry. If there was something amiss on the trail, Charley sensed the trouble long before Henry or the other critters. He'd stop dead in his tracks and start braying to high heaven. Henry said if Charley stopped, you'd better pay attention. There was an old cowboy saying most that also applied to Charley: "if your horse don't wanna go there, neither should you." Henry figured I'd be "plumb safe with Charley carrying my truck." With that in mind, we introduced Charley to Gus and Baily so I could leave the next morning.

I had been in California for some eighteen-odd years. During those intervening years, obviously, I hadn't seen Henry. I missed spending time with him. He possessed so much Nez Perce knowledge and he loved passing his wisdom along to anyone who wanted to learn. He had never married and as a result had no children, but he spent many spare hours on the reservation teaching children their language and heritage. He taught them how to work with horses, Appaloosas specifically because they were part and parcel of Nez Perce horse culture. The children (ages four to twenty) took to Henry's lessons like ducks to water. They loved and respected him and he returned the favor. Before I moved to California, Henry managed to teach me a thing or two as well. My dad and he had been friends for years and whenever dad had to leave for some work-related thing, he'd send me down to Henry's family so they could look after me. When I was older, after my dad died, I would go visit Henry whenever I had time off. I'd go with Henry to pack tourists into the backcountry . . . I had a blast, and Henry taught me more than just packing. He taught me about life, native spiritualism, and about man's connection to Mother Earth and all who inhabited the land . . . man and animals. We were like brother and sister. Now, all these years later, he knew something was wrong.

"Bret," Henry declared, "you are troubled. I can see by your expression and the way you carry yourself you are disconnected from Mother Earth. You have come home for healing."

I could never hide anything from two people in my life . . . my father or Henry. Now was not the time for pretense.

"Henry." I sighed. "I have been . . . I don't know . . . out of balance for a while now. I can't seem to find my center. Once I retired, I thought my problem would resolve itself . . . that didn't happen. I have been seeing a shrink for some time. He says I can't make a decision, I'm ambivalent. How's that for a diagnosis? He put me on anti-depressants, like that's going to do any good. I decided to heal myself with a good dose of home."

"Why do you think you are in this place?" Henry asked, knowing full well why.

"Too much crap," I said, "too much technology, too much stress, too much city life, and probably too much coffee. But I don't want to stop living near the city and I won't give up coffee. Once I moved onto the ranch, I thought I'd feel better. And that did help some, but I still felt something was missing, I was off center. I thought a trip into the mountains . . . a quest if you will, would help."

"I am puzzled as to why you went to a doctor," Henry mused. "Seems to me, Bret, you have diagnosed your problem. Only you can find your way. Only you can walk your path. Only you can find your center. Tonight you will purify yourself with a ritual sweat. You will relieve yourself of all the impurities in your system. Only then will you be ready to begin your journey."

Good old Henry. He sure did know how to cut to the chase and get to the bottom of any problem.

'Thank you, Henry," I said. "I value our friendship, truly."


FROM HENRY'S PLACE to Three Rivers (the confluence of the Lochsa, Selway, and Clearwater Rivers), took only a couple hours. The drive from the bridge to the trail head (on the Selway) would take another two hours . . . the miles weren't bad, the road was. After thirty miles of rump pounding miles, we arrived at the trailhead. I parked the rig out of the way, but where I could get out easily when we returned. I unloaded the animals, tied them to the trailer and started getting out the gear. I hadn't packed a mule in a while, but Henry's lessons were good and the procedure came back quickly.

"Well, there ya are, Charley, all put together and ready to go," I said. I gave him a scratchin' on the forehead and he leaned into my hand. Charley was an amiable animal and as most mules go, pretty nice to be around.

"Okay, Gus, your turn."

Like Charley, Gus was pretty affable and easy to get along with. Although he was still young (five), he was trained really well. He was good in the show pen as well as, most importantly, on the trail and in the open gathering cattle. I scratched him on the head, but he wanted more. He was rooting around for a piece of candy.

"Oh, my Lord," I sighed, "you are a chow hound and spoiled to boot. Here."

When Charley saw what Gus got, he wanted some too and made it plain. He brayed like there was no tomorrow. I turned to Gus.

"See what you got started? Now I guess I'll have to bring these along. Dang, spoiled rotten animals."

Whenever anyone goes up into the backcountry, the forest service asks you to leave a form that says where you're going, who's with you, how many, and when you expect to return. That just makes common sense. Back in the day, you only worried about animals, an accident, or maybe getting lost. These days not only do you worry about natural calamities, but crazies with guns as well. Who knew? You might stumble onto someone's illegal marijuana grow or a lunatic survivalist or two. Daddy didn't raise a fool; I was going in armed and I was a good shot. I usually hit where I aimed.

Just as I was leaving, a forest service ranger, on foot, came down the trail toward me. Might as well be neighborly, I thought.

"Howdy," I called, "nice day, huh?"

"Sure is," he replied.

"What's the condition of the trail ahead," I inquired.

"How far up are you going?" he asked.

"Moose Creek," I replied. There was no sense in telling him I was going to veer off the trail from there. My final destination was my business.

He looked over my animals and pack.

"Well, there isn't anything too serious. You may have to go around a deadfall or two and this time of year the trail might be a bit boggy here and there. Looks like you know what you're doing; that's a pretty tight load ya got there. You shouldn't have any problems."

"Yes, sir," I answered. "I learned from the best. Be seein' ya."

I headed up the trail when he called after me.

"How long do you plan to be in the back country?"

"Oh about a week to ten days; maybe a little longer. I want to make the most of my time. Don't get up here as often as I like."

"Really," he pressed. "You from around here?"

"Ranger Bob" was gettin' just a bit too nosey for my liking.

"Yeah, but I moved to California a few years ago. I best be on my way; I wanna get as far as I can before dark. Nice talkin' to you."

Dang! The whole point of this trip was to get away from people; I hoped there weren't a bunch of campers, packers, and hikers up here. I picked this time of year for two reasons: first, the rattlesnakes shouldn't be too abundant (the Selway is noted for the rascals) and two, people weren't planning vacations this early in the season . . . it was still pretty chilly at night in these mountains. I just hoped my planning wasn't in vain.

One good thing about going up Trail #4 to Moose Creek is that the trail is pretty easy going. The condition is so good because so many hikers and packers use this trail, therefore maintenance is pretty good. There was roughly twenty-six miles to cover to Moose Creek. Charley and Gus were in dang good shape so the likelihood of getting three quarters of the way there was pretty good. Besides, I was in no great rush. After all, I was on a quest of sorts; the idea of being in these mountains was to cleanse my soul so I just let the environment do its thing.

I couldn't have asked for better weather. The Selway can be really hot, but in early June, the temperature was around the middle to high seventies and once in a while up to eighty degrees. The animals took the weather in stride and we made good time. About twelve miles into our journey, a trail led down to the river. There was a wide place next to the river large enough to make a good camping spot for the night. As a matter of fact, I had camped here before with my nephews, many years ago. The river access made a good place to get water and there were trees close enough together to string a high line for Gus and Charley.

Both Dad and Henry made sure to impress upon me the importance of taking care of the animals first. After all, without them, I'd be afoot in short order and this trip would be a whole lot less enjoyable. I led Gus and Charley down to the river for a good long drink; Baily followed along and dove right in. She splashed and swam around Gus and Charley, managing to get them both wet. Not being one to let an opportunity to cause trouble pass, Gus dropped his muzzle into the water and threw his head back and forth and up and down until all of us were soaking wet. Charley voiced his displeasure by braying as loud as possible. If horses could laugh, I'm sure Gus would be.

For my part, I didn't feel like I needed a bath, but I got one. Time to go to the high line and get tied up, next to their hay bags, of course. I didn't bring hay, but hay cubes. Their bags held enough cubes for one meal without dropping anything on the ground. In the back country, there were strict rules about packing in anything that would become invasive. Cubes and grain would leave no trace that we were ever here, plus Gus and Charley love the cubes.

By the time I got camp set up, the sun was just about to set, and I was ready to feed myself and Baily. I only dug out enough supplies for one night, so dinner would be a little sparse. Top Ramen and bread would be our fare . . . Baily would eat her dog food. Of course, I had to have coffee in the morning. I had pills to drop in the water for purification purposes . . . the water looked clean and clear, but no one should ever take chances . . . not these days for sure. I found a good drift log to perch on by the river. With coffee in hand, Baily and I sat down to listen to the silence. No traffic, not planes flying overhead, and no electronics. The flowing water was soothing; I just sat there. I hadn't enjoyed this in years. I was amazed at how quickly I fell back into the spell the wilderness environment cast over me.

"Baily," I whispered. "Listen, you can hear Mother Earth talking to us. I know you have keen hearing, much better than mine, but I know you've never heard this before."

We sat there until dusk settled over us. Baily had never been in these mountains, and I think she was a little overwhelmed. Her ears were pricked the entire time we sat by the river. She watched, she listened, and she understood. I had taken her with me in the Sierras, but the Selway/Bitterroots are different. In deference to the folks in California and Nevada who think the Sierras are the be all and the end all; they can't hold a candle to these mountains. The Bitterroots are higher, more rugged and there are far fewer people who come up here. To the uninitiated, these mountains can kill you. These mountains almost killed Lewis and Clark. I know I'm biased; after all I was raised in these mountains, more or less. My childhood and early adulthood were spent vacationing in these mountains . . . I couldn't get my fill. I never knew how much I missed this place until I returned. With only a few hours here, I already felt a sense of renewal. I could feel a kind of re-energizing coming over me way down in my bones. But the best or worst was yet to come.

"Come on, Baily," I said. "Let's get ready for bed."

Baily had been trotting along behind me when I realized she had stopped. Her slight whimper made me stop too.

"What do you see girl?" I followed her gaze and there across the river stood a doe and her fawn drinking.

"Can't see that in the city, can you, Baily? Better than barking at squirrels, huh? C'mon, let's go."

There's something about fresh, clean mountain air that brings sleep in a hurry. I checked on Gus and Charley, banked the fire, and crawled into my bedroll. I knew Baily and the stock would wake me if something was amiss, but I slept with my pistol under my pillow just in case. Sleep was instantaneous.

Morning came as usual, with one exception . . . no traffic noise. Yay. The sun had not yet risen the above the ridge across the river and there was a distinct chill in the morning air.

"Dang, you guys," I said to the critters. "I'd forgotten how cold the early mornings are up here. Whoo hoo."

I threw some wood on the hot coals and soon I had a cooking fire going. I sat the coffee pot at the edge of the fire and set about the morning chores. The stock came first . . . they needed food and water. While Charley and Gus were eating, I gave Baily her morning meal. I dug out a frying pan and some bacon and eggs . . . my turn to eat. I was in no particular hurry to be on my way, except that I really didn't want to climb the steepest part of the trail during the midday heat. While the boys were in good shape, there was no point in making them work hard if they didn't have too. There would be plenty of hard climbs before this trip was over; I wanted them to stay as fresh as possible. I checked my watch when I mounted Gus.

"Hmm, eight-thirty," I remarked. "That isn't too bad. This isn't the earliest I ever got started, but not the latest either. Okay, fellas, and girl, let's get going."

BACK UP ON the main trail again, we made good time. Fortunately, there weren't many hikers or packers out this early in the season. Only a few hardy souls ventured out now. In early June, a freak snowstorm or two might happen and in the really high elevations the snow hadn't yet melted. From the end of the road to Moose Creek was a good twenty-six miles. That may not sound very far, but those were mountain miles and there is a big difference between that and flatland miles. I figured to keep up a good steady pace and along late afternoon, I'd make camp wherever I was at that time. Besides, I was enjoying being in these mountains again; I didn't want to rush to get where I was going and then head back. Ten days to two weeks was what I provided for; I was going to make the most of every second of every day. Long about noon, I heard a crash in the trail up ahead that made me stop in my tracks.

"Hold up there, Gus," I said. "Let's give a listen."

After the first crash, in about a minute or two, there was another, then another. There was just enough break in the foliage to see up ahead and over the bank to the river below.

"OMG, you guys," I declared. "Look at that."

Charley and Gus had their ears forward and snorted some, but they never moved. My brave dog cowered underneath Charley's belly.

"C'mon, Baily. You needn't be alarmed," I said. "That, my friend, is a herd of elk. Must be twenty or more. Either they are really thirsty or something up the mountainside must have spooked 'em. Don't worry, they aren't carnivorous. They're more afraid of us than we are of them."

They couldn't have been more than thirty yards ahead. In all the years I spent in these mountains, I'd never seen anything like this.

"Wow. Pretty cool, huh guys? Hmm, I wonder if I should mention this to Claudia," I mused. "You know the first thing she's going to ask is, 'did you take pictures?' Then I'm going to have to tell her no I had my hands full of horse and mule."

Dang! That is something I sure enough would have liked to document. Oh well, I will never forget my encounter that's for sure. Daddy always said if you fool around in these mountains long enough, you're apt to see most anything. I still had a nagging question as to what spooked them. I was hoping it wasn't a griz or a big cat . . . even up here, a little cat was nothing to mess with.

I eased Gus forward, hoping whatever spooked those elk was long gone. When we got to the spot where the elk had gone down over the bank; their presence was clear for all to see. A trail of tore up brush and busted up tree branches was strewn all over. They had cut a swath about twenty feet wide down the mountainside, across the trail, and down the embankment to the river. They swam the river and took off up the mountain on the far side; they never broke stride. Yes sir, survival of the fittest.

"Holy crap, you guys," I exclaimed. "If we had gotten to that spot five minutes sooner, we'd have been right in the middle of them. That would have been the end of us. Dang! Someone is obviously looking after us."

I dug out my field glasses and scanned the hillside above us. Whatever spooked the elk was gone, or at least well hidden. Hopefully whatever it was didn't have a taste for Appy or mule meat.

"Well, boys, if that doesn't get your heart pumping, nothing will," I remarked, to no one in particular.

I decided we'd better push on at a little faster pace. Since this was the second day out Twiddle Dum and Twiddle Dee had their second wind; I figured we'd make Moose Creek by late afternoon/early evening. I could eat lunch in the saddle . . . I packed all kinds of finger food and had plenty of water. I stopped occasionally to check Charley's pack and cinch for saddle sores; Gus's also. We made really good time and before long. The airport runway lay dead ahead.

"Here we are, guys, we're almost to Vista Creek," I said. "Finally, we're closing in on the reason for this trip. We'll spend the night at Vista Creek, then in the morning up Whistling Pig Creek. Henry said the first part of part of Whistling Pig trail isn't too bad. There are mostly game trails, but they're well defined. Henry said if we get to Shissler Peak, we've gone too far."

I guided Gus and Charley past the out buildings and found a place across Vista Creek in the trees close to the river. I had to admit, I was glad to be out of the saddle to stretch my legs. We had traveled close to thirty miles . . . mountain miles . . . which isn't exactly a walk in the park. I untacked Charley and Gus, then stretched a high line from a couple good trees. Before I tied them, I took them down to the river for a drink and a bath. I brought a sponge, a brush, and collapsible bucket along for a good grooming session. The river isn't too deep or fast flowing at this point, so both boys waded right in. I scrubbed and brushed until trail dirt and sweat was gone. After we got back up to my chosen camp site, I put the bell on Charley and turned them loose in the meadow so they could graze a while. There wasn't too much meadow, but there was enough to give the boys a good graze. Once they were taken care of, I set about my camp chores. Baily found a soft bed for herself under a tree on top of fallen pine straw. I figured why not. I laid out my bed close to, but not under the tree.

"Ya know, Baily," I chuckled, "lying under a tree in these mountains isn't the wisest thing. In case of a lightning storm, you don't want to be under a tree."

She just looked up at me, sighed, and laid her head between her front paws. She was one pooped pup. I let her ride on top of Charley's pack over the really steep, rocky places, but I have to give her credit. She walked, trotted, and even ran most of the way up here. She took off every once in a while to chase after a squirrel, chipmunk, or the occasional rabbit. I sure as hell couldn't have hiked this trail. Even riding, I noticed the thin air affected my asthma. Good thing I had my "whoofer." I figured she'd move over to me when I bedded down for the night. Again, because we were only going to be here for a night or two, I didn't drag out all the camp paraphernalia . . . just enough to get through the night. Naturally the coffee came out of the pack first.

I had to admit, this trip was just what I needed. I was really enjoying myself. I know none of this will resonate with most people, but I truly felt at home . . . as though I had become part of the environment around me. I knew my place in the universe; I was where I was supposed to be. Mother Earth was welcoming me back to our tribal traditions, back to my family. The feeling wasn't surreal; this was real.

I passed the evening sitting by a small cook fire, sipping coffee. Baily had gotten her second wind and went off exploring. Gus and Charley hadn't strayed very far away; they were peacefully grazing, guess they were tired also. I surely wouldn't have to hike very far to bring them in for the night. I had been taking pictures every chance I got, mostly to pacify Claudia. But once I began the last leg of my journey, there would be no picture taking. The place was sacred to the Nez Perce; the Great Spirit created the valley for them only. My duty was to care for this valley with great reverence . . .

I FOLLOWED THE river until I reached Whistling Pig Creek; I always wondered who named these creeks. There certainly weren't any pigs around here, particularly whistling pigs. Oh well. Henry was right; the first part of the trail wasn't bad, but then before too long the well-defined trail turned into well-defined game trails. There is a big difference between man-made trails and game trails. Generally speaking, Man-made trails have few breaks. If there is an obstacle, man removes the obstacle. With game trails, there's none of that. An elk or deer simply jump over dead fall or bogs . . . a horse and pack mule not so much.

"Okay, boys," I breathed. "This is where you earn your feed. Given our choices: jump over all this deadfall or go around, I choose to go around. How 'bout you?"

Around we went again and again, then straight up the mountainside. This went on for two or three miles. More than once, I dismounted and lead the boys over or around obstacles, like shale or granite hillsides. We stopped frequently to catch our breath. I was beginning to think this wasn't one of my better well thought out plans. When I was just about to throw in the towel, the trail leveled off and I saw what I was looking for. Whistling Pig Creek disappearing underground was what Henry told me to look for first. He directed me to follow the sun's path. The sun's movement would reveal the entrance. I can't tell you exactly how I was directed to the right spot, but suffice to say, I no longer laughed at Native American mysticism. Laugh if you want, but I swear I saw what I saw.

Once I walked through Mother Earth's door, the most beautiful valley spread out before me. I couldn't believe how this valley could be hidden so well. I mean even satellite photography couldn't reveal this place. I felt like I was in the Garden of Eden, if that really existed; maybe this was the place. At the far end of the valley, there was a beautiful waterfall that fed a small lake and the creek flowed from there. There was ample graze on either side of the creek, so the boys would be well fed. On either side of the valley walls, tall Douglas fir and cedar trees grew in abundance. I imagined the boys would be joined this evening by deer and elk who came down to the stream to drink. After I unpacked (for the duration) and unsaddled the boys, brushed them down good, I turned them out to graze. Baily was pooped again.

This is indeed a sacred place, I thought. The spirits are flowing all around. Baily and I sat down for the longest time without making a sound. I was simply mesmerized; I decided to wait until tomorrow to make my prayer circle the way Henry had instructed me. This evening, I'd spend time exploring the world around me. I walked along the stream; Baily trotted along beside me. My aches and pains melted away.

"I just can't get over the beauty and serenity around us, Baily," I said. "The Creator certainly out did Himself here."

I had taken off my boots and replaced them with my sneakers. I took my shoes and socks off, sat down on the creek bank, and dangled my sore feet in the icy cold stream.

"Owza, Baily," I shouted. "This creek is dang cold. But it sure feels good."

Despite my warning, Baily just dove into the creek. Fortunately for her, she has a good thick fur coat to insulate her from the cold. She splashed around like a young pup. When she'd had enough, she climbed out and shook herself dry . . . all over me. While I was putting my shoes and socks back on, I growled.

"C'mon, let's go see some more of this valley."

We walked along a game trail that led up and away from the creek. The trail was well-worn and easy to traverse; this must be the main trail for animals coming down to the stream to drink and graze in the meadow. I walked for quite some time before I broke through the tree line. The trail switch-backed above a craggy outcrop which made for an easy climb to the granite rock. Since I was way above the valley floor, I could see everything. I scanned the horizon. Across the creek, on the east bluff, at the very top was a rock formation. I could swear the rocks came alive in the setting sun.

"Well, I'll be damned," I breathed. "Grandfather, I should never have doubted you."

When I was a smart ass twelve year old (or there abouts), Grandfather told me a story about a brother and sister who were punished for their pride, arrogance, and lack of gratitude for the gifts the Creator provided. They were turned into rocks. (Of course, I thought Grandfather had lost his grip on reality.) The rocks formed a sculpture of sorts that depicted a hunter riding an Appaloosa and on his arm he carried a golden eagle. The bickering children were forever charged to watch over the valley in which the Nimiipuu would live for many generations to come. I'd always thought the story was a myth, a scary story to keep kids in line. So was the story true or was this just a coincidence? I figured the grandfathers simply made up a story to fit the rock formation. Whatever the truth, seeing this would certainly put the fear of God in someone. When the sun dipped below the ridgeline, the sculpture returned to being just a hunk of rock and I was brought back to the here and now.

"Okay, Baily," I said, "let's go back to camp, get the boys in, feed them and us, then get to bed. I'm going to have an interesting, mind-altering day (or two or three) tomorrow so I want all the rest I can get. Besides, this thin mountain air isn't doing much for my asthma."

The next morning, I took care of the animals, ate breakfast, then went looking for stones to create my prayer circle. The whole process was not very difficult, but the ritual had to be followed to the last detail. Because this ritual is scared to the Nez Perce, I can't describe what happens in detail. What I can say is the supplicant (me) is required to stay inside the circle without food or water; I would use burning sage as part of the ceremony, pray to the creator for guidance, and smoke the small quantity of peyote used exclusively in this ritual. Henry had given me a small piece of leather and a leather string with which to make a medicine bag. The bag, pipe, and sage were all that I took into the circle. After the smoke, I simply waited for the vision that would guide me and hopefully heal me at the same time.

What if there was no vision? Well, then there would be no healing. Henry said maybe the supplicant didn't begin their quest with an open heart. Whatever the case, I would soon see whether or not I'd be healed. With the pipe lit, I took a long draw of the peyote. In the process, I dang near choked to death. But once my breath returned and with a few more draws on the pipe, I was transported someplace far away. My last coherent thought was how strong this stuff was . . . holy crap.


THERE ARE PEOPLE who have "died" and then came back. Some people call this an out of body experience. I certainly hoped I wasn't dead, but somehow my consciousness was separated from my body. I was floating over the prayer circle observing everything going on below me. (Kinda like omniscient point of view.) My bodily form was still chanting the sacred prayers and rocking back and forth. I guess I was free to explore so I moved along with the wind. Eventually I found myself hovering in front of the sculpture on the eastern ridge. In my present state, there was no time construct; I wasn't even sure if any of this was real. Perhaps my body over yonder was having a dream and when I woke up whatever was happening would be over and done. Yes sir, that's what was happening . . . I was having a dream. Okay, now that that was settled, I could just go with the flow. I bet you can guess what happened next. Yep, the rocks came alive once again and a young boy and girl riding double on the Appaloosa stood before me. You gonna guess what came next? Yes sir, they spoke to me.

"You have come here looking for answers," Bright Eyes said.

"What makes you worthy that you should come here," Gold Eagle chided me.

"Hush, brother," Bright Eyes commanded. "Because of your arrogance and disrespect we have been turned to stone and forever separated from our people."

I was sort of disjointed . . . no pun intended . . . so what came next shouldn't have been a surprise. A calm, reassuring, but commanding voice rose above the children's argument.

"Even after all this time, you are still quarreling," the old man said. "Have you learned nothing from your punishment?"

OMG! My Grandfather's, grandfather's, grandfather . . . He Who Sees the Past . . . figures.

The old man spoke to me. "And you are still the cynical one, my child. Why do you believe only what you can see or touch? You have been too long away from the people. You have lost your way. You have strayed from the right path. The time has come to cleanse your spirit."

At this point, I had a tiny grip on reality. I felt I had to know this was a dream . . . this wasn't real, was it? Regardless of what my subconscious might have thought, I followed along with Grandfather as he instructed.

"Come with me, grandchild," He Who Sees the Past instructed. "The time has come for healing."

The old man told me to mount the horse he provided. There was no doubt I was dreaming . . . never could ride bareback, but there I was following behind Grandfather like I knew what I was doing. We rode for miles along the creek bank before the trail rose up into the mountains. How could all this land be hidden like this? Obviously, the Creator had planned that this place should be inhabited by a people who truly honored and respected Mother Earth and all she provided. Finally, we crested the ridge that rose above the entire valley. I could see for miles . . . even the Selway drainage was visible.

"The is the place the Creator has provided for our people," the old man said. "Look down into the valley; tell me what you see."

If the Garden of Eden actually existed, this would be the number one contender. In my trance like state, I was amazed at what lay out before me.

"Grandfather," I replied. "I see the people, the Nimiipuu. They are living just as the Creator wished . . . in harmony with Mother Earth. There is life down in the valley, truly."

Grandfather nodded.

"What else do you see, child?" He Who Sees the Past asked.

I looked over the valley and then past the ridge to look at the Selway River drainage. Although still wild, the handprint of modern man was obvious. Clearly, the land had changed dramatically from the 1850s. Even though still rugged and imposing, there was something missing. Something that was in this pristine valley wasn't out there. I didn't have an answer.

"Besides the presence of my people in the valley and the presence of modern man in the Selway, I have no answer, Grandfather. I see the people living as the Creator intended," I offered.

Once again, Grandfather nodded.

"You have your answer, child," The old man said, then vanished as quickly as he appeared.


I DON'T KNOW when, I didn't know how, but I was transported back to the here and now. My first conscious thought was how hungry I was. I was told Mary Jane gave you the munchies . . . I couldn't swear to that because I had never smoked, ever, until I smoked the peyote. My next conscious thought was that I was cold. I was only wearing my underwear and that stuff wasn't intended for outerwear that was for certain. All I could think was what the hell happened. Oh crap, I thought what about my animals!

"Baily!" I called.

Thank God she was okay. She bounded out from the trees with a squirrel clamped securely in her jaws. Well, I'll be damned. She always barked at the squirrels in our yard, but she had never gone after one before, let alone catch one.

"Hey, girl," I said softly, "whatcha got there? Now where are the boys?"

Before I started the ritual, I turned Gus and Charley out to graze. I had no idea how long I'd be out, so they would just have to fend for themselves. There they were; munching like there was no tomorrow. The sun would set soon; the boys could stay where they were for the next couple of hours. After I got dressed, I did go down to say hello. Gus raised his head and took a step or two toward me.

"Hey, big boy," I whispered, "looks like you survived on your own . . . like a mustang . . . for the last couple of days."

Not to be left out, Charley wandered over for his scratchin'.

"Charley," I said, "thanks for lookin' after Gus while I was 'away.'"

The first thing I needed to do was get a fire going so I could have some coffee, then some dinner, and then sort out all the crazy images rattlin' around in my head. Believe me, no one would want to get inside my head right now; I wasn't particularly too keen on the idea myself. The prayer circle caught my attention; when I started there was nothing inside save for a scrap of leather and a string.

"What the hell, Baily," I remarked. "These things weren't here when I began my quest."

Instead of the scrap of leather, there was a small bag tied up by the leather string. In addition, there was an arrow drawn in the dirt pointing up the valley. Clearly, any reasonable thinking person would take off in the direction the arrow pointed. Then again, would any reasonable thinking person come up here (alone) to find something lost?

The coffee was done and so were the biscuits and gravy. I sat down to eat and pondered who made the medicine bag and the arrow. Since no one else was around, I had to assume I made them myself while I was under the influence of the peyote. Cautiously I opened the bag. A medicine bag contained items that represented the wyakin (spirit helper) the individual saw in his/her vision. My bag wasn't heavy enough to contain a rock, so I was hopeful the items were cool. I know that sounds disrespectful, but I couldn't help myself. I was like a kid on Christmas morning ready to open presents.

"Okay, Baily." I sighed. "Let's see what we got here."

Baily seemed to be as curious as I was because she hardly kept her nose out of my hands long enough for me to open the bag.

"C'mon, Baily," I admonished. "Give me a break here."

Inside the bag were just a few items: an eagle feather (wonder how I got that), bits of horse hair, a patch of dog fur (sorry Baily), a small quantity of soil, a couple of pine needles, and some meadow grass. I had a pretty good idea why these things were in my bag, but I wouldn't be sure until I followed the arrow to see where it led. I had no energy to go traipsing off down a trail to who knew where. I was exhausted from the ritual; all I wanted was sleep. I got up to go get the boys. I'd like to think they understood I how felt, but more than likely they were just ready for their grain. In any event, they came trotting across the creek into camp, saving me the walk to go get them.

"Thanks guys." I laughed. "You have no idea how tired I am and where I've been the last couple of days . . ."

I looked them over good, then I looked into two sets of big, soft kind eyes.

" . . . but then again, maybe you do."

I tied the boys to the high line, hung their feed bags, and then crawled into my bedroll. I fell asleep to the sound of the guys munching on their alfalfa cubes, and Baily, with her head resting on my stomach, snoring contentedly. My last coherent thought was how at peace I felt and all was right with the universe.

I awoke so refreshed I thought perhaps someone changed bodies with me. I was so sure in fact that, when I got dressed, I went down to the creek to look at my reflection to make sure I was me. Wow . . . I looked ten years younger! Okay, maybe five, but younger anyway. Baily broke up my self-aggrandizement party by jumping into the creek. At least now I didn't have to take a bath. The icy water sure as hell woke me up; the creek was downright cold.

"Baily," I reprimanded, "I could have done without the shower, thank you very much. But, gee, you really have taken to the water. I never noticed you jumping into the pond at home. Were you going for a midnight swim? Let's go for a walk and see where the arrow leads."

We walked up the trail and sure enough, about a quarter of a mile there was another arrow. This time carved in the trunk of a huge Douglass Fir. At every quarter mile there were more. One scratched on a granite rock and another drawn in the mud near the creek bank.

"Dang, Baily," I mused. "Someone or something sure doesn't want me to get lost."

Altogether, we must have walked a mile and half when we came to a cave. Oh yeah, I thought. Every horror movie ever made has some fool following some markers or other that sure enough leads to a spooky old house or cave. Take your pick . . . I got the spooky cave.

"Okay, Baily, you're man's best friend." I laughed. "So as such, you get to go in first. If I don't hear any howls of anguish, I'll follow. What do you say? Hell, you don't have any idea what I said."

Hmmm, maybe she did, 'cause she trotted into the cave ahead of me. Course the dang thing was black as ten feet down and I had no flashlight or anything to make a torch. Well, let's see if my outdoors survival skills are any good. I looked around for a suitable tree branch. Found one, now something to wrap around that would burn . . . uh huh . . . dried tree moss might work. (Claudia said the stringy hair like strands was Big Foot hair. Hee hee.) I wrapped a bunch of the stuff around the top of the stick. Now all I needed was a little pine pitch and something to ignite my torch and I'd be all set. I jabbed the stick into the ground and found a couple of jagged edged rocks that might make a spark. After all, this always worked in the movies. And luckily enough a spark caught up in the dried moss and my torch lit up the cave bright as day. YAHOO BUCKAROO! Now let's hope this cave wasn't home to a cranky bear or snarling cougar.

Fortunately, there were no large carnivorous critters in the cave. The cave was huge, had a high ceiling, and went back for some distance. Pffffiiittt, I felt like Josh Gates in *Expedition Unknown*, except had no intention of doing some of the dumb stuff he did. There really wasn't anything too remarkable here: a cave is a cave is a cave. Just when I was about to give up and call this a wild goose chase, the torchlight shone on a recessed section of wall in the back.

"OMG, Baily," I whispered, "will ya look at that."

I had seen Native pictographs before . . . back home on the Grande Ronde River, but never anything quite like these. The ones back home were carved and painted figures that told a story about the people who drew them. These drawings didn't so much as tell about the people who drew them, but rather told a story, a myth about how the Nez Perce people found this place, a place where they could make their home. These pictographs could be thousands of years old. But because they were in a cave, protected from the elements, they were as fresh as though they had been painted only yesterday.

"Baily," I remarked incredulously. "Look at this. These drawings tell a story that is hundreds maybe thousands of years old. Let's see if I can figure this out. Good thing I learned to read using sight words rather than phonics. Okay, as far as I can tell, this is a story about an exploration or journey of some kind. There are horses, animals, and people here. There also seems to be a deity the people honor or pray to and a wise man who tells the story. The Nez Perce were a people who had an oral tradition, so I'm surprised there is a cave painting describing the events here. Of course, I'm no archeologist. No laughing now; I am a retired college professor, so I do have some brains."

The story told about two young people who were tasked with finding a place for their people to live. Hold the phone, here. This sounded a whole lot like the story about Bright Eyes and Gold Eagle. I read on and sure enough, the pictures told of two youngsters, a brother and sister, who argued about which one was better at finding a place for the Nez Perce to live. They argued to the point where Coyote and Fox had to intervene and create a contest so the children could compete against one another to find the perfect place for the people. I whistled sharply and sucked a deep breath into my lungs. Baily looked at me quizzically, cocking her head from side to side.

"Baily, you could not have known. This was long before your time, but Grandfather told me this story when I was a little girl. At the time, I thought this was a tall tale . . . a story to teach children the difference from right and wrong. Might I have dismissed this out of hand because I thought my people's beliefs were silly or outdated? I remember something from my ritual, in the end, something I saw. The people were living as the Creator intended; Grandfather nodded and vanished. That's it, Baily; that's the answer to my problem. I must live as the Creator intended. Could this really be that simple?"

Probably. I am always complaining about the fast pace of life. Whose fault is that? Life is what you make it, right? If my life is too hectic, then I have to be the one to change my life. Live "the way the Creator intended." Well, I'll be damned.


THE TRIP BACK was uneventful. We took our time and camped two nights between Moose Creek and Fenn Ranger Station. I was hoping I wouldn't run into Ranger Bob and have to have a blow-by-blow conversation about my trip, but then, on the other hand, I would be civil. I have to say, when the truck and trailer came into view, I was more than glad to see it. Fortunately, there was no one around when I tied up to the trailer.

"Well boys," I laughed, "we got here in one piece. As soon as I get you untacked and brushed down, let's go down to the river and get a good long drink, and then we'll head for the barn. Charley, I bet you'll be glad to see Henry and your home place. And Baily and Gus, we still have a long trip yet, but you'll be surprised how quick we'll be home."

After a three-hour drive, or thereabouts, Henry's place came into view. Boy, was I glad to see his smiling face. I thought I was in pretty decent shape, but a two-week trip like this sure took a lot outta me that's for dang sure. I wondered how Henry was able to keep this up at his age.

"Hey there, old woman," Henry laughed, "how ya doing?" Old woman was right. Every bone and muscle ached.

"I'm alive," I replied, "and that's about all. I swear just about all of me hurts."

"A good sweat and a soak in a hot tub will take care of that. While you're doing that, I'll fix you a good meal. How does a grilled steak, fresh corn, and a salad sound to you?"

"Good enough to eat, Henry," I said.

Why do we complain about technology? We say we need go back to nature? But we are all too happy to have technology after cell phones, etc. have gone missing for a while. Oh my Lord, was I ever happy to have hot running water and a bath. I felt almost human again. I wasn't made to be a mountain man. Contrary to my protestations. Henry had a nice meal and a glass of wine ready for me when my bath was done.

"You look almost presentable." Henry chuckled. "Smell a dam sight better too. Here have a seat and drink this. I have to say, this is the best year for wine I've had."

Did I happen to mention that, in addition to all the other endeavors Henry engaged in, he also had a small winery. His wasn't anything to rival California's wine country, his wine was nothing to shake a stick at either.

"Golly, Henry," I admitted. "Didn't you know I quit drinking . . . altogether . . . let's see . . . been about four years."

"Oh well, in that case . . ." He started to take the glass away.

"Now wait a minute, Henry," I said quickly, "as long as this is for medicinal purposes, I think the good Lord will overlook my backsliding."

We both enjoyed the camaraderie friends often share over dinner and good companionship. We sat outside in the cool June evening air. The fire crackled and the stars shone above as brightly as ever. Baily lay at my feet alongside Henry's dogs Bit and Rebit. (Don't ask me, I didn't name them.) Gus moseyed around the corral with Charley. Neither of us had spoken for quite some time. Henry broke the silence.

"Gee, Gus and ol' Charley have taken quite a shine to one another, haven't they?"

"Yeah," I snickered. "I always thought Gus was part mule. But, I guess no matter the species, man or animal, the Creator meant for everyone to get along."

Henry laughed, then said, "So, my friend. On this journey, did you find what you were looking for?"

I thought for just a moment. "Yes Henry, I did."

We spent the next several hours talking about my quest. Probably the most profound thing I learned was also the most obvious: never throw away your culture. You can never run away from who you are; perhaps you can lie to others, but never to yourself. In the end, when you are your most troubled, near defeat, the traditions of your people will pull you through.

The next morning, I packed up all my gear and headed southwest to the ranch . . . my new home. I'd been gone long enough and God knows what Claudia had done to the horse's manes and tails in my absence. As much as I loved the Lochsa/Selway Bitterroots, these mountains weren't my home any longer. I had carved out a new life for myself in California; there were people there who loved me and whom I loved as well. Two things for certain: if ever I needed a dose of my old home, I knew where to come and I had friends and family there who loved me as well.

T.K. Galarneau was born and raised in North Central Idaho in a small farming and ranching community called Nezperce where she graduated in 1969. She received a BS degree in English and History from Lewis-Clark State College in Lewiston in 1973. Terrie taught English and Reading in the Lewiston school district until moving to California in 2001 to continue her teaching career. She now makes her home in the Bay Area with two dogs, three cats, and two horses. When she's not teaching or writing, she spends most of her time riding.

Visit her website: http://bunkhouseramblin.weebly.com

Just aim your phone camera at the QR Code

www.ingramcontent.com/pod-product-compliance
Lightning Source LLC
Chambersburg PA
CBHW030639130626
46552CB00002B/933